Praise for *The Rosefields of Zion*

I was held in this book's spell from start to finish—transported to another time and place where author Marilyn Brown conveys just enough hope to tell a story of heartbreak, music, and heritage. There's a reason Brown is heralded as one of the great Mormon fiction writers of our time, and The Rosefields of Zion *proves her ability to retain that title.* —Josi S. Kilpack, author of the Sadie Hoffmiller Culinary Mystery series

Accomplished author Marilyn Brown . . . knows the formula for successful literature: a subtle plot with levels of meaning, an important site, and well-crafted sentences. Many legends of the park bring the locale to brilliant life. The writing is mature, crisp, and rich . . . a wonderful read! —Douglas D. Alder, president emeritus of Dixie State College, and author of *Sons of Bear Lake*

Fast-paced and well-written, The Rosefields of Zion *illuminates the Zion National Park area's legends and landscape at the same time it tells a page-turning story about a family in conflict with the U.S. government's urgent need to purchase their farm. A poignant fictional tribute to Southern Utah's breathtaking preserve.* —Veda Tebbs Hale, author of *Ragged Circle,* and biographer of *Giant Joshua*'s Maurine Whipple

Marilyn Brown is one of the Church's literary treasures. The Rosefields of Zion *is a touching story of a young woman's struggle to find love and happiness in the face of overwhelming*

loss and crushing circumstances largely not of her own making. If only we could all demonstrate such patience in suffering! —Elizabeth Bentley, Parables Publishing

The Rosefields of Zion *is a beautifully written story of a family and their fight against the federal government's creation of park lands in the early decades of the last century. Marissa, Michael, Carter, Morgan, Joey, their parents Ellen and Bradley, Blair Harper, Wade Keller, and all the other characters are totally believable and add an attractive dimension to this story that cannot fail to engross the reader. The plot moves convincingly to the story's rather sad but quite realistic ending.* The Rosefields of Zion *should be on reading lists everywhere.* —Alice D.

the Rosefields of Zion

Marilyn Brown

CURRAWONG PRESS

Currawong Press
110 South 800 West
Brigham City, Utah 84302
http://walnutspringspress.blogspot.com

ISBN: 978-1-59992-890-6

Acknowledgments

This book is much more fiction than history. Only a few of the stories are true. Mr. Behunin and Mr. Albright are historical figures. There really was a Jim Owen who shot the wild animals. Most of the "included" legends and their settings are actual, and I owe the historians, such as Angus Woodbury, Douglas Alder, Bart Anderson, and Lyman Hafen, many thanks for keeping the stories alive. It is true that there was a family who lived on the farm during this period (approximately 1912–31), but in no way did they resemble the Rosefields. Their name was actually Crawford, and they were famous residents of the area for many years. The fact is that they were finally forced to sell their land to the National Park Service in 1931 during the Depression—and for a Depression price. The grandmother, who loved living among the red rocks, was reluctant to leave and is on record as saying, "Just let me stay here until I die."

When stories are told and retold, they lose their authenticity unless someone is willing to set them into a format that will last over time. I am so grateful for the enthusiastic and dedicated people at Currawong Press who graciously worked with me to publish this book. Thanks especially to Linda Prince for her excellent editing, and Amy Orton for the perfect cover.

And many thanks to all of those working so hard to develop an exceptional body of literature about our experiences as a religious culture in the West.

One

When their mother Ellen was still alive, she sat her musical children down in the living room with their instruments—Michael with his bassoon, Marissa with her cello—and coaxed them to follow along as she played classical tunes. Father and the two oldest boys ignored them, coming back and forth from the barn, slamming the screen door. But little brother Joey clapped and sang with them from his playpen. Ellen was fairly good at the piano, dancing her fingers on the keys and turning the pages. When she heard Michael and Marissa play Debussy, she praised the duet. "It sounds good," she would say. "I love this phrase, and you did it well, both of you."

That was before she died with a blood clot that lodged in her brain.

Everything changed for the Rosefields. Ellen's death stunned all of them, but no one as much as Papa. In the middle of the night, Marissa could hear her father walking around the house in his leather slippers, *tap-tap* on the wood floor. She watched him sink into a place that seemed far away—another world.

In just those few days before the funeral, he seemed to lose his short-term memory. He lost the keys to the tractor, and the boys had to order the locksmith to drive all the way from St. George through the towering red canyon walls to make a new key. On the night before the funeral, Papa insisted on staying in his chair and listening to the radio.

At three o'clock in the morning, Marissa woke to hear heavy static. When she went out to the living room, Papa was snoring in his chair with the radio on an empty channel. Tiptoeing over to him, she just about bumped into Michael. He put out a hand to steady her. As he caught her arm, the old, heady feeling suddenly rose inside her. She closed her eyes momentarily to try to block it out. It had never gone away. It was wrong. It was forbidden. She gritted her teeth to dampen the flames.

Michael knew also, and he let go of her and put his fingers to his mouth. "Shh. I heard him too."

Father woke suddenly. "What . . . what?"

"You forgot to turn it off, Papa." Marissa's head spun from getting up in the dark, and from Michael's touch. She steadied herself. "We need our sleep. There's a funeral tomorrow."

But her father seemed to ignore her. "Both of you are awake? Then play for me," Papa mumbled. "That one your ma liked—the Dubby-see."

"Now?" Marissa said. "But Papa, it's . . . we'll wake . . ."

Without hesitation, Michael fumbled for the bassoon under the legs of the piano, opened the flannel envelope, took out his reed, and began to suck it. Marissa picked up her cello and tightened the hair on the bow, then drew the bow across the bridge of the instrument until the notes hung in the air and made such harmony with the bassoon that a phantom sang between them like a holy spirit. When the pair of tones flowed down the scale into the nether regions, they found vibrations that seemed to echo from the red stones: the Watchman peak behind them, Angel's Landing, and the faces of the monolithic Patriarchs, who might have been nodding their heads in approval.

"That's very pretty," Father said before his heavy eyelids fell and his graying fingers relaxed in his lap. "Very beautiful. And she is listening."

Marissa could see Michael's eyes in the dark. She fought another wave of feeling.

He stopped playing. "Marissa, can you go back to sleep? It's the funeral tomorrow."

She nodded, feeling the weight of all she had done to fight her tears, to stop her yearning, to create music in the midst of all that was crashing down around them, and to stay steady while she realized that Papa—his breath jagged in his lungs—was losing touch with reality.

Just as she wrapped her cello in the old blanket, Morgan and Carter stomped in from their rooms. Marissa wondered why they had finally come when the music was done.

"What's going on?" Morgan drew his hand through his ash blond curls, trying to push the sleep out of his eyes.

Carter peered from behind the doorjamb. He hid because he never wore pajamas. "You'll wake Joey."

From the dark recess of the distant lean-to room, Marissa thought she could hear Joey murmuring.

"Shh. Papa's finally asleep." Michael nodded toward the figure lying in the chair like a huge rag doll.

Marissa put her fingers to her mouth.

When the boys withdrew to their rooms, she stood with Michael in the shadows. She waited for him to leave, swallowing back the quick breathing that often threatened to begin when they were alone.

"Good night, Marissa," he whispered.

He had grown tall. His smile was a slip of a moon beneath the black eyes, the coal black hair, his coloring unlike any of the other Rosefields. "He's our little Indian baby," Papa used to say. But that was all he said, and it was laughed off as a joke. Ellen never moved her eyes, never let the muscles of her mouth pull away her smile.

"Good night."

Two

Because the two boys wanted to milk before 6:00 AM, they shook their heads angrily if they hadn't slept, sometimes tramping in and out with heavy feet. But Michael always walked softly to the barn on his milking day. Today was his day. "He always does things different," Father would say, a man unable to understand why a male child wanted to blow through a horn more than do much of anything else. But Michael seemed even-tempered about it, continuing to send his breath through the bassoon with a strong but consistent pressure, producing a sound pure and full. Michael had been Marissa's inspiration to play.

Papa said he would not drive the old Chevrolet to the funeral. He gave the keys to Morgan. "You must take over, boys. The farm will be yours now."

Carter looked up at his brother and sneered. "If the government don't take it over first."

Morgan glared back. It was a subject all of them had been unable to bridge without anger—the fact that in this year of 1925, since the railroad had been built from Lund to Cedar City, the busses had been bringing twice as many visitors as before. The roads were being paved, and the Union Pacific Utah Parks Company had purchased the Wylie tent camps. And now, despite the skepticism that a road could be carved through the rocks, the Bureau of Public Roads and the Utah State Roads Department were funded to begin the impossible project. The

Zion National Park was exploding. And the Rosefield farm was in the way.

Long ago the family had made a tacit agreement not to bring it up. When the silence became deafening, Carter blushed.

Papa drew up, plunged his hands in his pockets, and looked the other way. Perhaps he looked for Ellen. That was the direction he was going. And the family was slipping into something so different, it was unrecognizable anymore. "I'll get in the back of the car with Marissa and Joey," he said.

Most of the family held up well in the receiving line at the Springdale chapel. Bishop Chauncey Robinson, followed by his wife and pretty daughter Julie, shook Papa's hand for a long time, then leaned over and said quietly, "Bless you, Brother Rosefield." Papa's eyes filled with tears.

The bishop's wife said, "The Relief Society would like you to stay for dinner afterward. You will, won't you, Brother Rosefield? With your family?" And the beautiful daughter Julie, her dark, curly hair pinned back in silver barrettes from her peaches-and-cream face, smiled more engagingly than she had ever smiled at the boys before.

"Yeah. She waits until our mother dies to be nice to us," Carter snarled behind his hand.

"Carter . . . !" Marissa could see a wary look in his eyes. She glanced at Morgan, and she noted that Michael's head was down.

Behind the bishop's family, the little half-Indian lady from Virgin—who was so tiny she was almost dwarfed by the tall, regal Julie—finally ducked through. For a moment, no one in the line saw her. But after Julie had passed them, shaking the Rosefields' hands warmly for the first time in her life, Little Bird suddenly appeared like a leprechaun whose magic defied visibility. She could not have been more than five feet tall. Thin, with a sallow face that looked yellow more than red, she had wrapped her large, black braids around the crown of her head. She was wearing an old housedress made from a flour sack, and oxford shoes she had probably picked out of the Church hand-me-down barrel. Over her left shoulder she was carrying a large, colorful Indian blanket that seemed to drown her with its bulk.

"Be yours," she said, pulling the blanket from her shoulder.

Bradley Rosefield drew back. "What?"

"Be yours," Little Bird said quietly.

"It belongs to us?"

"Ellen want you have." Bird poked a finger from Marissa to the blanket and back again several times as though she were directing an orchestra. "Ellen old blanket. Now Marissa blanket. Wrap big fiddle in it."

Marissa looked at Father.

Bradley stiffened and stepped slightly away. "All right." He hesitated. "Thank you." His words seemed vacant of any feeling.

Marissa knew that if they brought the blanket into the house, Papa would not touch it. Perhaps what bothered him was the animal hair, the insects imbedded in the wool, or just the fetid odor of old native campfires that burned long ago before it was named the Mukuntuweap Park. The Indians wanted a life for a life, he told his children. Papa had told several stories of encounters with the Indians—tales that curdled Marissa's blood. Tom Flannigan, for example, shot an Indian out of fear, and they wanted his life. It was only fast talking that allowed the ranchers to give the natives an ox in exchange. In January 1865, Papa's own father had gone with James Andrus to hunt for the stolen sheep of Whitmore and McIntyre and found one of their arms lying bloody in the snow. Grandpa told of the massacre of Robert Berry, his brother Joe, and his wife Isabel in revenge for the death of a native family that had stolen a settler's beef and sat eating it over a fire. Old Hyrum Stevens from Rockville had been shot by an Indian in his youth, and Cyrus Hancock had been shot, though he outran the three marauders who continued to chase him.

Bradley Rosefield knew all of the grim tales. He had lived through them. But Marissa had only heard them, and could see the beauty of Bird's offering. The colors of the blanket were spectacular—gold, yellow, the green of sage, and the red of Indian paintbrush. It was blended in vertical rows separated by navy strands of soft wool.

Marissa realized she was holding her breath. "Thank you, Bird. You are so kind."

"I help you. Need mother now," Bird said.

Bradley drew back. "Oh, you needn't worry about us," he said. Reluctantly accepting the blanket didn't mean Papa accepted Bird. He had never let her come into the house. "She can stay outside," he had always insisted. "You give them an inch and they take a mile." He often recited the story of Orson Pratt, who bought the land where Rockville stood. It was owned by the old Indian Shunes, and called Shunesberg for a time. Pratt paid him well in cattle and doodads, but Shunes was never satisfied and continued to hang around Rockville all of his life, begging for food.

Marissa saw Papa's eyes mist over and watched him look across the crowd. This was a very hard time for him. He also seemed out of touch with reality during the meeting. Though he responded with tears to the bishop's kind eulogy, he seemed vacant at the gravesite. And it was obvious Papa was not truly present for the Relief Society dinner and the comforting gestures of the members who put their arms around him. Perhaps he was trying to connect with Ellen. Or in his mind he was going on one of the long walks he liked to take alone in the canyon, finding solace in the shadows of the red walls he loved. He was not ready to deal with others—even their kindnesses.

But as the days passed in so much distance and silence, there were many times Marissa thought about Bird's offer to help. She would have liked someone to come in and just talk to her about her mother. Leaning over the sink, Marissa would cry tears of exasperation because she remembered things about her mother that she could not talk about with her father: Why did Mother have so many different kinds of saucers but no cups to put on them? What was that recipe for the soft rolls? Did she always peel the pears when she dried them?

Bradley would not listen to questions about Ellen. He left the farm to the boys more often than he had ever done before. He took food in a little sack and, accompanied only by the dog, hiked the river and the canyon ledges. The absence of the mother was still like a mist hanging in their rooms, or floating over the red rocks in the canyon, and it was a cloud of sorrows and mystery Marissa could not seem to penetrate.

"We must listen for Ellen," Father would say to every question. "She will talk to us through the veil." There was definitely a veil, but it seemed heavy and opaque, like the wool on an old Indian's loom, oppressive and ponderous. And it seemed no surprise several months later when their father hobbled into the house from a harrowing fall on the Watchman. He had fallen before, but this time seemed much different. After Doctor McIntyre set several bones, Bradley still would not get up, even to hobble, but sat in a wheelchair they furnished him, unmoving on the front porch, looking at the red stones and hearing unusual music in the wind.

Marissa was concerned. While the boys worked the farm, she spent hours with her father, tapping into his memory, encouraging him to talk, to grasp some thread—any thread—from the past that might bring him into the reality of the present. He was still obsessed with the floods, the construction of the steep road and the bridges, and what all of this activity meant. He asked himself how they could have stopped the crowds coming into the canyon. Now he heard the truck motors and the rock grinders, when during those first years he could always hear silence and wind.

The canyon made music, the music Michael duplicated with his bassoon. Often on those evenings under the stars, Papa interrupted their talk, raised his hand, and insisted Michael fetch the instrument. "Do you hear it? It's the same pipe in the distance." Papa leaned forward, probably hearing the clear sound of the wind or spirit passing through some fissure of stone or tight bank of dry leaves. When Michael played, the wind answered with a vibrant, parallel resonance—the sound of a native flute. He still listened for it now, though it had not returned its echoing knell for several years.

Three

When Marissa was twelve, and all of them heard the song of a pipe vibrating between those high red crowns of rock and the water that whispered between them, she believed an Indian princess was playing. When she heard her father say, "Someone is playing the flute in the canyon," it sounded like a fact. She did not know he was pulling anyone's leg. He wanted Michael to play, and perhaps that was his way of insisting. The other boys joked along, but Marissa believed. And finally, one day, accompanied by her twelve-year-old curiosity, she decided to find the old flute player in the wind.

She was brave at first, traipsing out in the middle of one afternoon with a pail of her mother's applesauce cookies. Marissa would never tell anyone what she was doing because Morgan and Carter would laugh at her. Michael would smile, but she would be embarrassed if she did not find anything. So she just left a note: "Going upriver, back after dark. I took food. Don't worry."

It was on an afternoon when Papa and the boys were in the barn organizing hay bales for the winter. Ellen had taken Joey to Springdale to sit while she made quilts for the Relief Society.

Would Marissa ever tell her father what had happened on that day? He knew some of the details. But he did not know it had changed her life forever.

At first she followed the riverbank north. The cookies were gone when she sat on a rock and the shadows began to climb the walls of the canyon. She couldn't hear the flute. But she swore it was somewhere close under the weeping rocks near the emerald pool. Papa said this area had belonged to a Mr. Heaps who ran cattle along the range, until eight years ago when the railroad people met the Utah Park people on the muddy roads that sucked up the wheels of their busses. They'd put the convicts to work and built a passable wagon road to Zion.

People from the outside world had started invading the park long before the Rosefields had come. First, Major Powell, followed by Clarence Dutton, who finished the U.S. geological survey. But visitors began to come in earnest in 1904 when an article in *Scribner's Magazine* printed Mr. Dellenbaugh's oil paintings that were exhibited at the World's Fair in St. Louis in 1904. People wouldn't believe that what he painted was real.

Bishop Hirschi was there in St. Louis as a young missionary, and when he heard the viewers say the red rocks were a lie, he got up on a bench and told them otherwise. A whole crowd gathered. Not two years later, on June 8, 1906, Gifford Pinchot sponsored a bill that allowed President Roosevelt to set aside some parks. Grandma and Grandpa Rosefield, with some trepidation, watched the crowds increase when President Taft established Mukuntuweap National Monument in 1909. When Mr. Albright, the assistant to the National Park Service, came to insist there would be no more cattle grazing in the park, Grandma and Grandpa wondered what was happening to their area. But they tried to smile and welcome their visitors graciously. And Mr. Albright had been impressed, saying that the farmers of the area were cheerfully cooperating, so the government issued the orders that were "generally obeyed, with the result that the grazing was stopped and the shrubs and wild flowers in the canyon began to come back." He also added, smiling, "I shall always remember with keenest delight my early association with those good Mormon people, who, without knowing what a national park was, cooperated so fully in executing orders that brought them real hardship."

Grandma and Grandpa certainly did not know what a national park was. They called their area "Zion," because the first farmer, E.C. Behunin, who lived there from 1862 to 1867, had exclaimed at the canyon's beauty, "At last we have reached Zion!" Brigham Young was pretty perturbed at that boldness and set them all straight. "This isn't Zion," he told them. Zion was not a place, but a state of being. But the name wouldn't go away. For years they called it "Not Zion." But of course the government, just as they rejected the name Deseret and called the state Utah, rejected the name Zion and called it what John Wesley Powell had heard the Indians say—"Mukuntuweap," which meant "Straight Canyon," or "the place of the Gods." That was in 1917. But in 1919, after months of confusion, Secretary Mather agreed "Zion" was all right, and on November 19, 1919, President Taft signed the park into official existence. By then, with the government's large boots ever stomping on the ground, most of the cattlemen like Mr. Heaps, and his buyer Jennings, had left the area, and Grandma and Grandpa Rosefield left the farming to Bradley and Ellen, and passed away.

Though Marissa had heard the stories many times while her father walked the river with them, she always learned something new. And though she had seen all there was to see of the red rocks, glassy water, and golden leaves, she was always surprised at the beauty of their world—the steep walls that closed out the light. Grandmother used to joke that when the sun went down behind the Patriarchs, the canyon darkened so much that the dumb birds thought night was coming. But when it didn't come, they got tired of waiting and poked their heads out again.

That afternoon the darkness seemed deeper than usual, and the leaves noisier and thicker. Marissa thought she'd heard something, but it sounded like dripping water. She tightened her fingers around the handle on the pail.

Through the leaves she thought she saw a roof. She knew Mr. Heaps and Mr. Jennings had grazed their cattle somewhere along here, but she didn't know there was a shack by the river in the woods under the walls. Ahead of her, through the shimmering leaves and the close branches of little willows standing along the edge, there was a dark blur—a crude little cabin with a heavy sod roof woven with sticks so old they looked like white bones.

It was a cabin that had survived the flood. *The floods.* They were another matter. Marissa had so often heard her father talk about the worst flood of their lives, in which they almost lost the three boys. Fortunately, the two older boys, Morgan and Carter, had been pulled from the stream, but the baby Michael, born that year of 1908, had been lodged by the powerful water in the crosshatch of logs and broken branches. Luckily, Ellen found him before he drowned in the foam. The Rosefields thanked God every night for years that their children had been spared. But there was a story mixed with legend that the little half-Indian woman Bird, who lived in one of the abandoned cabins with her daughter and new baby, had not been so fortunate. She lost both her white lover and their baby in the flood. Grandpa Rosefield said she was still waiting for her family to return.

For a moment, Marissa stood wondering if this was the little house where the mysterious Indian lady still longed for her wild lover to return with their child. She wondered if the woman was still here, playing her sad flute, or if she lay in the cabin, dead.

Marissa thought briefly of turning back with the empty pail. But she was sure she had found the origin of the flute playing that harmonized with Michael's bassoon. So she stayed fixed like a lamp post, leaning to one side or the other until she had the courage to go forward a few steps—until she thought she saw movement on the other side of the little house. Prickles went up and down her spine.

After a steady moment, she allowed her feet to move forward again and felt the pail bounce against her knee.

The door was open. The inside of the cabin was black, like a rabbit hole. Marissa came closer and closer, wishing she had brought more cookies. When she was nervous, she liked to eat.

From the doorstep, she was surprised to see a little chimney on the north side of the shack, and a little pile of crooked rocks with a couple of empty spaces where stones had fallen to the ground. There wouldn't be any smoke, because it was still summer.

Inside the cabin was a cupboard with one Kerr jar of what looked like bottled cherries, sparkling in the faded light. In the far corner sat a chair and a small table. The chair had a big ladder back, and paintings on its slats of little Dutch girls in blue bonnets. In the other corner of the cabin was a bunk bed with old quilts thrown on top of it.

Marissa knew she shouldn't go inside, but she did. And when the door shut, she was never sure if it was the mysterious Indian who played the flute, or just the wind that shut it. But the door shut, and when Marissa tried to open it, she could not.

For a moment she sat on the ladder-back chair, but she didn't feel like leaning against the paintings of the little Dutch girls. She thought about what she ought to do, or what she could do. She looked in the pail and thought to herself, "There are only a few crumbs." There were no more cookies, so she could not eat. But she could not help but gaze at the jar of cherries on the shelf. The point of light that struck it came from the only opening—a foot-square window in the west wall. The window was surely not a way out, for it looked like heavy glass that would not break no matter how hard she might try. And she did not want to break up someone's house.

She waited and tried the door again, but it would not open. She wasn't ready yet to scream or holler, because she wasn't sure a tourist could hear her over the water above, dropping like a hundred little waterfalls from the weeping rock. And she knew the ranger in the lodge only a few blocks southeast was much too far away to hear any sound she might make, big or small.

She wondered if her oldest brothers, Morgan and Carter, on their way back from carting hay to La Verkin, would drive up this far into the canyon. It would probably be Michael—almost fifteen now—who would discover her note, or look around at the empty house and ask, "Where is Marissa?" She was glad she had written that she was "up the creek," because she certainly was up the creek now. When someone discovered her note, at least the person would not be going in the wrong direction.

Marissa would have to wait—something very difficult for her to do. She lay down on the bed. When her stomach began rumbling, she gazed at the bottle of cherries, which she knew would save her for a while from starvation. The light still passed through them as though they were alive in the jar. She picked up the bottle and turned it, watching tiny spheres of fruit moving in the liquid. Just to make sure they were a possibility, she grasped the lid and tried to turn it. It was tight. But when she hit the top of the jar lid with the corner of her pail and then tried again, it opened. She drank some of the juice and let a cherry or two float into her mouth. They were delicious. She spit out the pits.

This was the longest twilight she could remember. She decided to send her thoughts to Michael like a telegraph. So in between cherries she concentrated on it, curling up on the bottom bunk and sending out spirals of light to his brain. Marissa thought about his brain, his head with short black hair on the top like a lawn mower went over it, his sliver of eyes when he smiled, his pointed chin, his grin like a Cheshire cat. And when he blew into the bassoon she concentrated on his cheeks that puffed up and changed everything about his face as he wrestled with the instrument. Music was Michael's connection with the earth—the way he communed with the breeze and the mystery of its magic—as though he had only a short time left to find the secrets of the red stones and of his own life, as though there were something he wanted to talk about and there were no words to say it. And so he had tried to blow it, hoping it would materialize into something tangible he could put his finger on, and it would be understandable to the world.

She didn't know how long she slept. But she was awakened by a bobbing light and a faraway voice. "Marissa, Marissa."

She leaped up when she heard her name. She knew it was Michael. She scrambled to the door with her feet still tangled in a dusty quilt.

"Mi–chael," she called.

The shadows in the little house danced with the moving light through the darkness, changing the way the dying sun came through the glass brick window and down the chimney.

"Ma–ris–sa," Michael called. Then there was scratching on the door. It was Rumbo, their German shepherd. He was clawing and making a fuss at having found her.

When Michael was close, he said, "Marissa, let me in."

"The door slammed shut, and it won't open."

There was silence now, except for the sound of clutching and pulling on the latch. Michael jimmied it.

"Now that they've moved the old Indian, they should tear this hut down," he said through the door. But there was a crack and it opened. Emerging in the light of his lantern, Michael was a white face in the dark. "There, we got you."

"Michael, Michael!" She ran to him and leaped up to him, throwing her arms around his neck. "You came!"

She held so fast to him, he straightened to back away. But by then he was so close to her, he was breathing her breath.

"I smell . . . flowers?"

She released him and grabbed the jar from the table. "Cherries. Try them. They are so good!"

Michael peered into the glass jar, took it in his hands, and tipped it. He smelled it. "You had some of these?"

"Taste them." Marissa jumped up and down and clapped her hands. "They saved my life."

"You don't die in one day." Michael laughed at her. But he put the bottle to his lips and tasted the cherries. Then he took a longer draught.

"I'm so glad to see you!" Again she jumped up against his chest and clung to him, until he put the bottle down on the table. And this time he responded to her. He leaned over her. And then something happened that she would never forget. He put his arms around her. He held her. And the room whirled.

There was silence. Neither of them had ever stood so close to one another before. Neither of them had guessed they would ever feel so close to each other. And something seemed to open up in the room around the lantern Michael had set on the table. Through the noiseless pine rafters and the beat of Rumbo's tail against the edge of the chair where he sat panting from the long walk, something bloomed like a faraway light.

As Michael bent over Marissa, some exchange happened that pulled them apart to look at one another with startled eyes.

When he spoke, his voice seemed deep inside some kind of music that usually came from the instrument he played. "I feel . . . like I want to kiss you." He paused, for only a beat. "But it would be wrong."

Marissa tried to ignore the pounding of her heart and the explosion in it that threatened to stop her tongue. "You kissed me before."

"Yes. But not . . ."

She tried to breathe, then pulled back from him so she could see him. "Maybe . . . maybe."

He pulled away and glanced around the room. "Do you know where we are?"

"The house where the old Indian lady played the flute?"

"She was half Indian," Michael said. "It was Heaps's cabin first. The government took over. They never saw her, but they put packages of food on her doorstep. They finally had to move her to a house in Grafton."

"What happened to the daughter who lived here too?" Marissa asked.

"They say she has a job in St. George," Michael said, his words almost eaten up by the beating of Marissa's heart, the sighing of the leaves, and the noise of the weeping water.

"An Indian girl. Who was her father?"

"Maybe a white man. They say her mother lived with one of the hunters who killed for the preserve."

Marissa knew that when President Roosevelt established the Grand Canyon Natural Game Preserve in 1906, he invited professional hunters into the area who killed eight hundred cougars, five hundred bobcats, eighty wolves, and three thousand coyotes. Papa Bradley had been nervous because he believed such defilement would upset the balance of nature. Bishop Robinson had asked him, "Is there ever a balance? What do you think we have done to the Indians?"

Marissa remembered hearing Grandpa Rosefield, Wade Keller, and the square-dancing instructor talk about the history of Zion's Indians. Once the family of Paiutes, called Parrusits, lived along the river. But only a few Shivwits lived west of Santa Clara now. No Indians but the Indian mother in the Heaps's cabin had ever lived in the canyon. When E.C. Behunin came as a Mormon pioneer in 1862 and said, "This is Zion!" his Indian guide would not come into the canyon. The native escorts always waited outside because they believed there were dangerous spirits here. And most of the Indians agreed the canyon was haunted. If the little Indian lady paid attention to the legends, she must have been very brave to live in the shadows of the ravine.

"Perhaps she believed the flood punished her for having a child with a man who killed the animals," Michael said. "I heard she also believed the father took the baby to the Superstition Mountains and disappeared."

At that moment Rumbo got up from the floor and knocked his nose against Michael's leg as though saying, "What are we waiting for?"

"Do you know who that Indian lady was? It wouldn't be Bird by any chance, would it?" Bird was the only Indian Marissa knew.

Michael drew back. "Bird? I never thought . . . No, I don't think so."

"I was hoping I'd find the one who plays music with you," Marissa whispered.

When he smiled it brought light into the room. "You been listening to me play with the wind?"

"I love it when you play."

"It's just wind, Marissa," Michael said. "There's nothing to it. There is just music of the canyon. Just air. But I like to play with it because it's something no one else has ever done."

For a moment they stood apart, as though if there were a possibility to capture the moment in the quiet darkness, they would fall into each other's arms again. But of course they did not. They stared at one another as though that instant they had discovered what had passed between them had stabbed them with the point of a dagger. And the edge of the knife was heavy with too much pain.

"You like my music. I didn't know you listened," Michael said softly.

She saw him smiling in her mind's eye, though she could not see his face in the dark. "Thank you, Michael, for coming."

"I read your note. And when you weren't home for dinner I guessed something was wrong. I came as soon as I could."

"You came at a good time."

"They need to burn this place down."

Outside the door, on the path, Rumbo stood ahead of them, his tongue hanging out, his eyes glassy in the light of the lantern.

That evening at the house, Papa wanted Michael to play in the dark. When the family sat outside in the yard, watching the stars, something different came down among all of them. Something strange and strong. Though she was only twelve, Marissa knew what it was. She and Michael were like one person. She was clinging to her heart so it would not explode.

She was relieved when Michael bolstered his instrument under his arm and carried it out into the reverberating slabs of sandstone, to suck on his reeds for a minute or two and answer the strange canyon flute with the voice of his breath. While the family relaxed under the canyon's circle of stars, they listened to Michael answer the pipe playing in the distance—a sound like the talk of two rare birds who know they are in the presence of each other but can never meet face to face.

Four

Only recently, when Marissa played the cello, would she lug it to the porch, tighten her bow, and play the few notes that would bring Michael back from the empty hills. The two of them joined in the strange harmony that seemed to soothe Pa's thoughts. His thoughts needed calming—to be lulled away from the fog that accompanied Ellen's death. But the fog seemed to lift less and less. And the day Papa's hiking ended in a serious fall was the day the air grew so dense it crowded out all of them until it was difficult to breathe.

No one knew what he was doing when he fell. The mechanic, Wade Keller, who had been fixing the truck, had been walking at the foot of the Watchman on his way back to Springdale when he heard the faint moaning. He had rummaged around in the blackberry bushes and found Bradley lying in a thicket, his face scratched and his bones broken.

For the three days after he fell from the Watchman, Papa lay on the bed. His gray face seemed illuminated as though the shafts of light slipping through the massive red canyon were playing him like music. Though he lay silent for only three days, it seemed like forever.

Between cooling his cheeks with ice packs, stirring the gruel, bringing his tea, changing the cumbersome pads beneath his unresponsive body, and talking with Dr. McIntyre, who bound his bones but seemed unable to do anything else for him,

Marissa wearied and knelt at the bed, rocking and holding his hand.

In and out, the boys came into the room with long faces, all with question that had no answers. The broken rake? The brindled cow? Where was the paint for the shed?

Marissa nodded mechanically, unable to answer any of their queries, sometimes sobbing, cursing the death of her mother not long ago, the rocks of the canyon, the Watchman, and the reef formation where her father had fallen. "What were you doing, Papa?"

Before he had lapsed into half consciousness, he had whispered, "All week . . . heart cramps. I was getting the papers. The key. I didn't tell you . . ."

"What key? Getting the papers?"

"Watchman."

"Where on the Watchman?"

But Papa's hand had grown clammy and he had grabbed her fingers and clutched them so hard the excruciating pain of his own torture seemed to leap through her in an unexplainable way.

Marissa released her fingers from his hand and ran to the yard, calling to their hired repairman, Wade Keller, who was banging the wrench at some echoing metal under the hay truck. At Marissa's urgent words, the hammering stopped, and she heard the mechanic slide out from under the truck onto the weeds, lumber to a standstill, and mumble something before his feet pounded the dry roadway to the barns to fetch the others.

In his last breath, Bradley did not say goodbye. He did not open his eyes to look at his sons standing before him as pale as ghosts. He babbled something about a key. "The key."

"What key?" Marissa leaned over his gray lips so close she could hear the sucking sound of his lungs.

“Barn door.” He wheezed.

Marissa glanced at the boys, who stood like crumbling pillars at the foot of the bed. All four of them had been in and out for three days. But there had been cows to milk, horses to feed, hay to stack. This morning she had warned them to stay close to the house—to try to limit their activities to the barn or the corral—or at least stay somewhere nearby. For several days they had watched their father turn his head to the wall. When all of them finally reached the room, they waited in what seemed like interminable silence. Even the mechanic stood behind them, fingering his greasy hat. Marissa could sense Wade’s breath, as though he were standing over her shoulder. Joey, still a boy, stood beside Wade, clutching the hay rake as though propping himself up so he could see.

“Barn door?” There were three barns on the property. “Which barn? Key to what?” Marissa tried to keep the anguish out of her voice, but it was quickly boiling up.

She glanced at the others. They looked at each other. Shrugged. “We don’t know about a key on the barn door,” Morgan said. He had come into the house sopping the sweat from his cheeks. The brassy curls on his neck caught the light from the sun.

Because she had been hovering over her weak father for three days, Marissa’s body seemed to have separated itself from her mind. She did not think they missed anything. They had gone over all of the instructions carefully. They must heed his wishes: the property must never be sold—especially to the U.S. National Parks for the expansion of Zion. They must maintain the dam. It was all right to sell stock and purchase cedar in St. George. It was all right to sell the horses—they would make good glue. There was a rendering outfit in Scipio. “Sell them while they can still trot. Use the truck, but scrape the roads level to keep the ruts from beating the axles to pieces." All of the boys said they had heard everything for several years. Marissa felt the whirl of the dictates crowd her thoughts. She clasped her father's bony claw in her fingers.

"Flood . . ." He halted. There was congestion in his throat.

What about the flood? But that was all they finally got out of him. Somewhere there was a key. It may be hanging on a barn door. It was the key to something Bradley had buried, and he had never mentioned it before. Then his head lolled to the side and he sucked up his last air. The rattle in his throat was audible even to Joey, who raced to his bedside and threw himself over the quilts and buried his face in his father's shoulder. His sobs shook his body so hard that Marissa came to put her arm around him to keep him from shaking the bed.

"Flood." She sank to her knees and covered her face with her hands. She wondered if what she was feeling was panic, or was it her father's last word that sliced into her memory with the power of a whip? She had heard the story of the flood for many years. Had her father wanted to talk about the flood, perhaps because it was one of the most traumatic experiences they had suffered? The young Rosefields, Ellen and Bradley, lived in the flood plain. Ellen had been picking watercress in the ditch when the water came down that morning. It was the same morning Papa Bradley went to town to talk with the government agent, Elias Workman, about the land the U.S. National Parks wanted to buy for the park. Boiling up suddenly like a monster, the water had swept the children before Ellen and took the baby out of the wagon where he was lying. The water slammed the two older boys into the trees below, where they clung to the branches, and she found the little baby, Michael, lodged in a cluster of debris.

On the following day, the town had come to help put their lives back together and found little socks and tiny shirts hanging on the stalks of dry weeds and old tree limbs. Ellen had clung to the branches with her arms around Carter and Morgan, praying fiercely. She had watched the bodies of other children floating downstream. How she had saved her sons, and baby Michael, crying in a nest of sticks and stones, she did not know. She had credited God and rejoiced that her children lived.

Marissa parted her hands to look at her father, then smoothed the wet strands of hair away from his brow. He was still warm.

She looked up at the boys. Their pale faces stiffened with fear.

Five

For several days after the funeral, it was quiet. One day, at the end of a long week, Marissa woke in the light and saw a bird at her window. The creature did not fly away, but stood looking in at her with an ominous eye. Marissa lay back down on the bed and looked at the ceiling. Something must change in their lives. Some light must chase away the darkness.

That afternoon, she made a cheese soufflé. For the first time in a long while, it stayed tall in the oven and came out in a perfect dome that didn't fall until the boys trampled through the door.

"It smells good," Michael said. He smiled his singular smile, the one unlike any other in the family. When he gazed at Marissa, she glanced away.

Morgan and Carter seemed glum, so she said, "It's time we stopped this gloom. Let's remember the good times. Papa and Mama are looking down—they would be happier if we smiled."

Joey's chair screeched when he pulled it out without lifting it across the floor.

"Yikes!" Carter squawked.

Marissa slammed her eyes shut. Two noises were not better than one.

"We think . . ." Morgan paused.

Marissa stopped on her way to the table with the falling soufflé. "We think?"

"Do you think it's too soon to go . . ."

"He wants to go to the dance at the church," Carter belted out. "He thinks Julie Robinson would dance with him."

Carter had a way of spinning things. He had said the last words with a slight sneer. Marissa knew in her bones that both boys had been encouraged by Julie's warmth at the funerals, and Carter had been coveting Julie for himself.

"Mama and Papa would want us to be happy. But also," Marissa said, "we need to be kind."

She set the dish in the center of the table, and after the prayer no one mentioned Julie again.

"I saw two men in a Buick," Joey said.

"Two men?"

"What two men?" Carter asked.

"I saw them too," Michael said, his hands on the table.

"Was it a black Buick?" Morgan wondered.

"Yes," Joey said, his mouth full of cheese soufflé.

"The government." Carter snarled.

"What did they want?" Morgan asked.

"Just had some yellow flags."

"Yellow flags?"

Marissa sat back in her chair. "They are surveyors."

"The government wants to buy the farm again. They're breathin' down our necks. They want to see our papers," Morgan said.

Marissa looked across the table and across the room through her brothers.

"Where are the papers?" Michael asked.

"I think Father was trying to tell us that before he died," Marissa said.

"The will." Carter sat forward. "It's in the box with the key. He said the key's on the barn door. I think he took the box to the Watchman."

"That's what he was trying to take care of when he fell," Morgan said.

"He buried it high to protect it from the floods," Carter added. "But now . . . how are we going to find it?

Marissa saw the light fade behind the windows over the kitchen sink. The dusk was breaking up streaks of magenta over the canyon walls. She remembered taking walks like her father did, walking along the river and picking up the brittle shells of snails that used to lie along the bottom of the Lake Bonneville. She did not know if the water had come this far south, but she believed it had. Sister Flanigan had mentioned it once in Sunday School class, drawing it on the blackboard. And Marissa had asked the square-dance instructor and schoolteacher, Mr. Blanchard, if he knew anything about it. He had rubbed his palms together and said, "No one knows exactly how large the lake was. But millions of years ago it must have covered a big stretch of the West here, because I've found those snail shells everywhere on the tops of the mountains. Could be billions of years old. There's horizontal lines up by Salt Lake City, where the water must have lapped on the shore once, then dried away into the Great Salt Lake, leaving little streaks like the strata of old rocks. I think the water dug out this red canyon we live in, and all we got left now is a trickle. But every once in a while it floods like the dickens."

Remembering this bit of speech by Mr. Blanchard, Marissa thought about how many times lately he had called the square dances on the basketball floor at the new chapel built not too many years ago in Springdale. She had heard that a rehearsal for one of those dances was coming up on Friday. The Rosefields seldom went to the Church dances, but now she could see a hunger in her older brothers' eyes that looked different from anything she had ever seen before. Carter had a little worried tension carved into his lean cheeks under the dark curls at his ears.

“I think we ought to try to find that box.” Joey’s voice interrupted Marissa’s thoughts. She shifted in her chair and looked at him. He was at that age when adventure seemed more important than anything else. He hadn’t liked haircuts and could barely see through the sun-bleached curls that hung over his nose. He had Morgan’s rough hair streaked with gold, and a straight nose and almond-shaped blue eyes. At barely thirteen he was large for his age, with strong, rounded shoulders and big hands. “Can’t we go look for it?”

Marissa brought herself back from her musings.

“We have to look for it,” Morgan said. At twenty-two, the responsibility for the farm rested on his broad shoulders. He was bigger than Carter by half a foot, his upper body stacked with muscles, his legs long and lean.

“Well, I’ll go,” Joey offered. “I think I know where it was buried.”

“You don’t know nothing.” Carter shook his head. “Nobody knows where he buried that box. The Watchman is huge.”

Marissa stayed silent, thinking the chances of their finding the box were as good as finding the proverbial needle in a haystack.

“There’s an office in St. George that keeps all the records,” Michael stated.

The boys turned to him.

“The county recorder . . .”

Marissa looked at Michael with the same eyes she had remembered seeing on him that day he came to rescue her from being accidentally locked in the cabin under the weeping rock. She had been a little drunk on the cherries she found in a jar in the cupboard. She knew she had lunged at him. She’d hugged him around the neck so hard it had sent them both spinning. For years now she had tried to justify that embrace—never had she been so grateful to see anyone in all her life. But the memory of holding him so close had changed her life. Something unexplainable, powerful, hung between them like the sound of a bell that keeps ringing in the countryside, echoing down the hills forever, and refuses to stop.

"Well, I think we should climb the Watchman and take a good look before we deal with any government office," Morgan said.

What was Papa thinking? Marissa wondered. He had been walking all over Zion for years. He could have hidden everything they owned anywhere along the canyon walls. No one would ever have found it. But should that "no one" include the family? He must have known how hard it would be to search the canyon for a shallow hiding spot unless he told someone where it was.

Mama must have known. Papa had finally told them where the key was, and they had found it on the back of the barn door. But the box? *He forgot to tell any of us,* Marissa said silently to herself over the cheese soufflé.

Joey asked Morgan if he could get up from the table. Without Papa it was the eldest brother he asked for permission, though the young man seemed reticent to take on that role.

Morgan nodded.

"What ya gonna do?" Carter asked. "Climb the face? It takes forever to go up the long way. You're short. You'll need the ropes and the hooks—them hook things."

"You'd better not go alone, Joey," Marissa interrupted. "Someone should go with you."

"I'll go with him," Michael said. But he wasn't smiling. He glanced at Marissa. "Will you walk us to the face and stand watch in case anything happens?"

"This is the stupidest . . ." Carter sneered. "Oh my gosh. You don't know where he climbed, or where he buried that box. It could be stuck in a hole in the rocks."

Marissa silenced him. “At least we’ll try. We know where he fell, and it’s probably up above that place. We’ll explore every avenue before we go to the office in town.”

“Well, you’re going to the dance tomorrow night,” Carter said.

The silence that followed was as weighty as the boy’s pronouncement.

“There’ll be time enough after a trip to town to go to the dance,” Michael said.

Marissa felt a wave of cool air on her cheek. Joey had already opened the door.

Six

Whenever Marissa went out of the house and stood on the doorstep facing the hills of Oak Creek, she breathed the air as though she had never breathed it before. It rushed into her with a burst of force. And because the afternoons were darkened by the shadows of the rocks, the atmosphere was always silver with expectation. It hung in the balance between the canyon walls like a huge spider web.

Michael wanted to go down to the road, but Joey said no. It would be best if they took the beeline through the blackberry bushes. Joey had done it so often that now the clusters of leaves had begun to part like the waves of a black sea. "Wade walks that way sometimes," he said, "and I walked it enough. You can see the dirt."

Marissa hesitated. But to be a good sport, she consented to go if they would wait for her to change her shoes. She had adopted a pair of Papa's old boots. They were huge, but she had put wool socks in the toes, and the boots would be impervious to blackberries.

The brambles did not begin until the three hopeful investigators passed the cabbage fields and the cantaloupe south of the barn. They skirted the cabbages. Joey led the way. Marissa followed Michael, hoping the boots would not rub her ankles raw, hoping she would not lose them under the huge mountain that loomed ahead like a ship at sea.

When the bushes began to thicken, some of the branches of blackberries rose up like the talons of predatory birds to prickle her eyes. She had her eyes almost entirely closed when she bumped into an obstacle. It was Michael—her face was in his shirt. The wave of feeling always came over her quickly, like a fever.

"Oh, he stopped," Michael said.

"What happened?" Marissa asked, backing away quickly.

"Someone else is using Joey's trail."

"Oh my gosh," Marissa whispered, still too close to Michael to erase the power of what had happened by accident. "Who could it be?"

Michael had stopped long enough behind Joey that Marissa could not see around a bend.

"Oh," Michael said.

"Oh, what?"

"It's only Wade."

"Our mechanic?"

"Yes."

Marissa wanted to peer around Michael, but she was trapped on both sides by the blackberry thicket, and she would not step more closely into Michael, with her heart pounding—with the danger of what she had felt for so many years. She had to bite her tongue to stop the hammering.

This was Wade's way back to Springdale if he had to walk. If his old car was running, he drove up the road. But he often surprised the Rosefields, walking to their place without notice, because he remembered the tractor had a clackety gearshift, or there was trouble with the differential on the truck. Stocky and solid, with a neck so thick he resembled the chef on one of Marissa's salt-and-pepper shakers, Wade was never one to say much to the Rosefields, even though he attended both funerals, and served as their mechanic before their mother died.

"Joey's talking to him," Michael said.

When Marissa and Michael moved closer, she heard Wade say, "There is two government guys here pounding stakes in the ground, and they was askin' me some questions. I got off the trail to show 'em what I thought was the end of your property."

Government guys?

"They're surveying again," Michael whispered.

"Well, did you tell 'em it goes to the foot of the Watchman?" Joey was saying.

"I told 'em," Wade said.

By now Michael and Marissa had come into view, and Wade looked up at them as though he expected a party in the middle of the thicket—as though at any time a bassoon, a cello, and a couple of bass drums would appear.

"What are you doin' here?" Wade's question hung in the air.

Joey hesitated. "We was takin' a hike."

"Nice evenin'," Wade said, obviously not believing him.

Tension hovered in the air so thick, Marissa could almost breathe it like smoke. Something was wrong, but she could not put her finger on it.

"Well, I got an appointment with Bishop Robinson," Wade said. "His carburetor. Excuse me—I got to get back on the trail."

He was going to plow through the Rosefields, plant his big feet step by heavy step as he pushed the blackberries aside. When he passed Marissa she could smell the grease in his dark snarls of thick hair.

"I don't trust him," Michael whispered when Wade had gone.

"He knew about the box," Marissa said.

"You think Wade would . . ." Joey began.

No one answered Joey.

“If the government men are still over there, I don’t think we ought to—” Michael said.

“If they are, I don’t want to run into them,” Marissa agreed. “Perhaps we should try another time.”

Joey followed Wade, slipping by Michael and Marissa. The trek back through the blackberries seemed shorter. Marissa and Michael followed Joey, who clanked as he went, the metal pins on the climbing ropes breaking against each other like castanets. Once the three siblings were in the cantaloupes, then the cabbages, Marissa breathed more easily.

“Something’s wrong,” she said. “Did you believe him?”

“I don’t know,” Michael replied.

“There might not have been anybody there, really,” Joey said. “Maybe we should go back and see for sure.”

“Just keep going?” Michael said.

“Yeah. We shouldn’t give up easy.”

“Reminds me of that James Holt who trekked the meadow canyon route and found a big piece of gold,” Michael said. “Maybe he shouldn’t have.”

“Shouldn’t have?” Joey said.

“When he got back to his house a stranger in white stood at his door and said, ‘Don’t look for gold.’ Then the stranger dissolved into thin air.”

“Where did you hear that story?” Joey asked.

“Grandpa Rosefield told it to me on the day we found the bones. And the next day he died. He never went back to the meadow canyon. People swore it was sealed up by an angel.”

“You think an angel might have sealed up Pa’s box?” Joey wondered.

Michael gave a laugh. “I think we ought to try some other ways first.”

“I hate to bother the county recorder,” Marissa said.

“That’s why they make legal records,” Michael replied. “To keep things straight.”

The sun had dipped behind the Patriarch peaks across the road. Dusk fell into the orchard like blurred ink, covering up the red rocks that stood ahead on the trail, burying the blackberries, the path, and the watching mountain. The pipes in the canyon began to blow.

Seven

No matter how much they tried to ignore what was going on outside their world, if the government men came on the property, the Rosefields knew it, felt it, as though it were that circle around the moon that promised a storm.

While Morgan and Carter argued over whether or not they should sell the farm if the National Park paid them a great sum for it, Joey backed out of the kitchen.

"Where are you going?" Marissa asked.

"Just want to take Rumbo for a walk."

The big collie padded across the pine floor when he heard his name.

Marissa spooned up the apple cobbler and put down the dessert dishes. She stood behind Carter and laid a hand on his shoulder when he said, "But do you know how much property we could buy with seventy thousand dollars, and then collect rents the rest of our lives?"

She gripped his collarbone as though to ask him, "Didn't we make an agreement with our father?" She looked at Michael. His eyes met hers.

"No!" Morgan slapped the table with his palms, making the apple cobbler leap. "We are not selling this property to the U.S. of A. to make an entry for the Zion National Park. I don't care how much money they offer us—even if it's enough to buy the Empire State Building."

Joey backed out of the door.

"This is our lives," Morgan said. "You don't sell your life for money."

Joey heard the last of his brother's words trail into the sound of the wind. He shut the door quietly behind him.

"You don't sell your life for money" echoed in his ears. This land was their lives—every cliff, tree, rock, and speck of sand. The very dust moving through stems and leaves that fed their blood. Joey was *made* out of this place, and he didn't think they ought to let go. He wanted to stay here forever. If only he knew where that box was. He grabbed a length of willow as the dog panted at his side.

"But we won't be here forever," he remembered hearing his old grandfather Rosefield say on that day before he died. On their walk to the Watchman, Joey stumbled on an old bone sticking up like a rotten tooth out of the earth. Grandpa Rosefield leaned over and dug it up. "Well, look at this, Joey. Some old Parrusit fellow, maybe fighting for his territory, dropped his bones right here."

Joey was six years old when he and Grandpa Rosefield discovered the bones together. And now they must add to this earth the bones of Joey's mother and father.

"What are the Parrusits?" Joey had wanted to know.

"Parrusits means 'diggers.' The old digger Indians," Grandpa'd said, fingering the sharp edges. "Their bones made the melons that made you. We're all out of this ground." He paused. "Someday maybe somebody will find our bones."

"Didn't they put them in a box?"

Grandpa brushed the red dust off the bone. "Probably dropped right here pullin' an arrow out of his quiver, and somebody else pulled one first." He gazed at the grooves in the white femur, ran his thumbnail along one. "Inevitable these bones would rise up out of the earth. Not all together, as in resurrected human beings with shaggy hair and straight white teeth. But these bones was here a long time, I wager." Grandpa was having difficulty communicating, and Joey could tell he was immersed in thought.

"How come we haven't seen them before?" Joey wanted to know.

"They just come up here finally."

The bones had risen up like live things, stirred up in the ground by the floods, by animals searching for buried seeds, and by horse hoofs and the edge of the plow. The bones were now appearing in pieces and in filtered dust that blocked out the sun.

"These bones wanted to talk to us," Grandpa mused.

"What they want to say?" Joey asked.

"They want you to pay attention to where you come from, and pay some attention to your own bones that will be risin' up someday."

Joey touched the edge of the bone with his fingers. "Is there more bones comin' up?"

"Probably." Grandpa started walking, carrying the bone in his hand. "But it would have to be around here, because the Indians were afraid of the dark places in the park. They were afraid of the spirits that haunted the rocks. Like a black cloud, the great evil lived in the tops of the monoliths. So they lived here where we live. They liked your farm the best. They probably died fighting tooth and nail against their invaders."

"Invaders?"

Grandpa looked at Joey sideways as if to make sure he was listening. "At first other Indians. And then . . . those invaders . . . were . . . us."

"Us?"

"When we came, the Indians left." Grandpa looked off in the distance. "You didn't see any Indians lately, did you?"

"I saw Old Pawgits, remember?" Joey said. "And there's Bird."

"Well, yes. We took care of Bird and made a house for her in Grafton. Old Pawgits was alone. He was why they named his place Pocketsville, and he believed it was his. He stayed while everyone else moved on."

"I saw him on the river."

"You were lucky. Not many saw him," Grandpa said.

Joey remembered well that wizened old Indian who seemed as red as the rocks around him, and who usually stayed hidden. He walked up and down the river to spear otter. He lived in a dugout along the Virgin. Before the flood, and before he disappeared forever, he hid in the rushes when the Rosefield boys came near. But when Joey was little, he had seen movement in the mesquite. And one afternoon that summer, when his brothers and sister Marissa had gone with Father to Washington City to sell hay and buy trousers, Joey crept up on Pawgits at the pond in the river. He watched the old man sharpen the stick and plunge it into the water, bring up the otter, skin it with a pocketknife, and lick the blood from the knife.

Joey hadn't said a word, but stayed as quiet as he could. While he watched Pawgits, a blue heron with a wing span taller than Joey himself swooped onto the pond.

Pawgits also saw the bird, and he must have heard Joey's quickened breath, for he glanced back into the brush, his black eyes wide with surprise. Without making a sound, the Indian set all four of his fingers up against his mouth, curled himself into a ball, and rolled under the brush. Not a whisper could be heard across the water except for the ruffle of the heron's wings.

It seemed like hours that Joey watched the bird preening and eyeing the movement under the pond. Pawgits watched, too. Finally the heron leaped into the air, spread its magnificent wings, and sailed across the mouth of the canyon into the dark recesses where sometimes there was not even a sliver of light.

When the Indian left his spot under the bushes, he came to Joey as though he were walking on all fours. Although he was upright, he came bent over like a small animal, dark and quiet, without shoes, with nothing on his head but strands of ratted hair and leaves. For a moment Joey was terrified, but there was no time to retreat without the danger of being rude.

"Gaw," Pawgits murmured. "Go!" He waved Joey away.

Joey saw him often after that. He kept many vigils at the river, and often jumped up and down waving his arms, hoping the Indian would look his way.

Finally, after Pawgits became used to seeing the boy, he beckoned to him to come to the edge of the water. And one day he invited him to sharpen a stick. He broke a long, straight branch of mesquite from a tree, pointed to his knife, and put it in Joey's hand. Joey made his own spear, and they caught some of the small trout in the stream. Pawgits ate them raw, without ceremony or preparation.

On his next trip that week, Joey found a few extra matches in the house, and took them when no one was looking. He helped Pawgits build a small fire under the overhanging rock near the dugouts that Mr. Hinton had built in the side of the riverbank so many years ago.

Joey and the Indian did not talk to each other. But if they had, Pawgits might have told Joey about the crumbled shelters along the river that once housed some of the "invaders" who had chased out the Parrusits. And he might have shown anger toward the Rosefields for being the next invaders—just as the Rosefields were watching the men who tramped the new roads with their big boots and planted short pieces of wire with little orange bits of cloth on top. The government officials came in 1909 to step off the edges of the park, and they were still not satisfied. They hoped to swallow the rest of the land. They wanted the Rosefields to sell their property for a visitors' center. Nothing stayed the same.

These days, the "invaders" were curious tourists who had come all the way through the park from the East Entrance and swept the area clean of artifacts. Even Flanigan's cable, built on the side of the hill to haul timbers down into the sawmill, had been dismantled and the rocks and lumber used to reinforce the concrete of the Hurricane canal.

Grandpa had told the family many times how he had admired the entrepreneur David Flanigan, who imagined and built the cable to haul lumber in 1900. The young Flanigan had been only twenty-seven years old. He was only seventeen when he watched the mail go up and down from the west side to the eastern heights on a wire, and said, "Why can't we go up there, take down all the trees, and send them down on wires?" It took fifty thousand feet of strong cable, and several fearful experiments to perfect the operation. The first live victim to go down was a terrified dog. On July 28, 1908, two young men coming down with their dates on the platform lost their lives when it was struck by lightning. Both of their girlfriends lived. Quinby Stewart sent melons to the bottom. And Frank Petty, who weighed three hundred pounds, offered to go down. He would have fallen to his death if his son had not stopped the motor in time.

But Joey didn't understand all of this until later. Just last winter, after his eleventh birthday, his oldest brother Morgan drove him in the truck every day to school in Springdale, and Joey lost contact with Pawgits. When school was over and the boy went back into the delta, Pawgits was nowhere to be seen.

Grandpa said Indians knew when they were going to die. They would lie down on the ground and let the Great Spirit take them up into the sky. The breath of the land was filled with the spirits of dead Indians who would gather their bones about them someday and speak from the red hills. At least that was what Grandpa Rosefield had told Joey. No one need worry about the Indians. They died in peace.

Now that he was fourteen, Joey could hope, but he did not know for sure if his father's spirit was at peace, swimming somewhere in the air with the Indians. When Joey had looked at the gray face in the coffin, he thought he could still see a great deal of pain in the wrinkles around the eyes, in the tilt of the brow. He believed it was because his father had left things unfinished. There had been the halting words about the papers hidden somewhere on the Watchman, but it was a huge mountain and no one knew exactly where they were. Yes, they had found the key that went to the box Papa had taken to the mountain. Perhaps that box was what he had been trying to get to when he fell. He had probably buried it high because everything they had once gathered together with their labor had been washed away with the flood.

On this evening, when Joey trekked to the edge of the property where the government was fastening little orange flags, he pondered the impossibility of investigating each level of the imposing slope. He thought about his father's face in the coffin, the mouth that would no longer tell. After they shook the hands of the bishop and his pretty daughter, after the women had finished holding his sister Marissa in their arms and urging her to accept their help, after they put Papa's coffin in the ground by the side of their mother's grave, dedicated the grave, sang the last songs—after all was over, Joey slipped away when he could and looked up into the Watchman to see if there was some clue to help him find his father's box.

Eight

At breakfast, when Morgan and Carter announced they were going to take the truck into St. George and purchase lumber to repair the shed, Marissa toyed with the idea of riding along with them and stopping by the recorder's office. And while she really didn't want to talk to the government people, she felt curious as to what they would say. Learning about Brother Blanchard's rehearsal for the Gold and Green Ball that same day, she was willing to think about risking her afternoon.

"You can go with us and see the recorder while we get the lumber," Carter said. "We'll be back to Springdale in time for the four o'clock rehearsal. Morgan and I decided to be in the dance group."

"Oh?" Marissa examined their faces.

"Are you surprised?"

She was glad they planned to participate, but she guessed why. "You're really serious about Julie, aren't you?" She smiled.

"No, that's not totally it," Morgan said. "You yourself said Mama and Papa would be happier if . . ."

"I know." Marissa poured a bit of syrup into her oatmeal. "It will be good, but there's always more girls than boys."

"But it wouldn't hurt you to go and see."

She hesitated before asking, "Is Michael playing?"

"They have a record player with a certain tune to dance by." Carter tore off his mud boots at the door and shoved his feet into his loafers. "But Michael said he'd do it too. He's taking the tractor into town, and he promised to meet us."

"So, if you're going to go with us to St. George, do you want to put on a dress for the dance rehearsal, and we'll stop in Springdale on our way home?" Morgan asked. He brushed the dark lock of hair out of his eyes.

"And Joey?" Marissa said.

"Joey will be all right. Won't you, Joey?"

"Sure," he conceded, plowing into his cereal. "I have chores." Almost inaudibly he added, "And things to do."

"All right then."

Marissa ate only three bites of her oatmeal. It took a minute for her to find the lawn dress and the straw hat with the blue ribbons. And it took her five minutes to dress and follow the boys to the car.

She never tired of the drive along the gravel road, of watching the hills in the distance fade in multiple layers of black, purple, and blue. She loved this land. It gave her such joy to watch it opening into the valley below—a panorama of green and red under an azure sky. She wanted to live here always, to stay breathing the pure air, to watch the hawks write calligraphic messages over the hills.

When Morgan and Carter dropped her off, Marissa stood for a moment in front of the courthouse to gather her courage. The building sat on the north side of St. George Boulevard, backed up against the slopes to the steep pile of red rocks that loomed above the city like huge slabs of rosy cherry fudge, smooth, cut, and shoved together, ready to be packed in a courtier's gift box. She had never climbed to the top, but she knew there were wide expanses above the place, fields and fields of sage, and arroyos dotted with mesquite and colored stones. Someday she would find herself on the top of this world, looking out over the expanse that lay before it, feeling the urge to fly.

The courthouse was a handsome Victorian structure with a cupola on the roof, a proper porch with white pillars, and a bank of steep stairs. Marissa hesitated before she climbed the front stairs, and again before she opened the door. The high ceilings emitted the light, and inside the front hall she paused to absorb the airy breath of the late summer sun on the light gray walls. A pleasant face met her at the reception desk. A small plaque was inscribed "Mrs. Harriet Montgomery." Mrs. Montgomery wore a floral-print dress with a white collar. And eyeglasses. When she peered over the glasses, she pressed her chin upon a second chin that led to a freckled breast. She was sitting next to a large photograph in a cherry-wood frame that featured a giant family, probably the Montgomery family. And if Marissa could have found Harriet in that huge crowd immediately, she would have known the truth about this woman. But there wasn't time to look.

"May I help you?" Mrs. Montgomery asked.

Yes, Marissa wanted to know if she could speak to the county recorder.

"Mr. Harper," Mrs. Montgomery said, glancing upstairs. "He's upstairs in the judge's chambers at the moment." She paused. "He'll be down soon. May I tell him your name, and what it is concerning?"

"Rosefield. Marissa Rosefield. We have not found our papers yet." Marissa hesitated. "And we would like to get copies."

It was not long before Mr. Harper made his entrance. When she saw him for the first time—when he descended the staircase from the judge's chambers—she would have to admit that it surprised her. She was expecting an old man. He came in a white shirt that blinded her eyes, and a vest that clung to a slim waist. His light brown hair was slicked back in the latest style above his wide brow and aquiline nose. When she saw his face, she searched it to find anything that would suggest he had the competency to take care of the records of any part of the United States of America.

"Hello," he said to her while she was still standing near Mrs. Montgomery's desk. "And you are . . ."

"Marissa Rosefield," she got out.

"And how may I help you?"

Mrs. Montgomery must have seen something in Marissa's glance. "Mr. Harper is new from Washington D.C. He and his colleague, Mr. Scott, have been appointed by Chairman Albright to redo all of the recordings in Washington County. He can show you almost anything. Right?" Mrs. Montgomery glanced at Mr. Harper.

He laughed. "Almost anything." He tipped his head enough to dislodge a wisp of the perfectly coifed hair that fell across his eyes. He indicated with this gesture that Marissa was welcome to navigate her way to his nearby office, where answers to "almost anything" would be given.

Turning to the west, they faced a wide archway. Behind the desk in the open room, a heavily made-up woman smiled with the same smile Mrs. Montgomery had given. But perhaps it was a one-grin-fits-all smile, for when the woman saw Marissa, her eyes dimmed just a little, and she glanced at her boss as though to question him. Her glance was practically buried in the waves of her blond curls, but her blue-green eyes were brightly visible beneath the coarsely painted eyelashes. She looked at Mr. Harper with a kind of questioning urgency.

"This is Bruzy," Mr. Harper indicated offhandedly. "This is Marissa Rosefield," he told his employee. "Bruzy is our receptionist. She came with us from New York and the offices of Washington D.C."

Looking past a partition behind the desk, Marissa saw dark eyes.

"And . . . come out, Tessie," he urged. "This is Tessie, who does the filing for us."

For a moment Tessie did not show herself. But at Mr. Harper's request, she finally lurched forward. As dark as Bruzy was light, Tessie looked almost like the receptionist's shadow. Her high cheekbones were flanked by thick, shiny black braids slung back like heavy ropes over her shoulders. Her wide lips were almost rust colored, as though she had just come out of the rocks at the top of the hill. Unfortunately, with her step forward, a stack of papers in her arms spilled out on the floor, flying apart in an explosion of white and yellow.

"Oh, I'm sorry, Mr. Harper," Tessie cried out. With fear in her eyes, she knelt to the floor and began to shuffle the papers into her fingers. Her braids fell forward against her cheeks.

"Tessie is . . . a graduate of the LDS Business College," Mr. Harper said, as though to assure Marissa that in no way had they hired what looked like a clumsy ox.

The commotion brought another man from behind a back cubicle. "What have we here?" he said, knitting his black brows. He was much shorter than Mr. Harper and wore a navy vest with a gold watch chain.

"This is Clarence Scott," Mr. Harper said. "We are redoing the records here. This is Marissa Rosefield."

Marissa thought she saw Mr. Scott's eyes snap open wider.

"So, you are one of the Rosefields?" He pulled back and put his thumbs in his vest pockets. "We know where you live."

Wary, Marissa said nothing. She removed her straw hat and glanced at Mr. Harper.

He smiled. "You're known at the recorder's office. Come in and we'll talk."

The door to Mr. Harper's office lay to the left of Bruzy's desk. It was not easy to dodge the papers Tessie had spilled on the floor. The girl looked up with a stoic expression that flickered with a hint of fear. But once they had skirted the papers—although Mr. Harper did not skirt the papers, but simply stomped over them as though an accident of this sort happened every day—he opened the inside door and led Marissa into a larger office facing the front, graced with a high south window that flooded the room with light. Outside, the leaves of bushes and trees tapped the panes of glass. A maple desk stood near the window, surrounded by rows and rows of large document folders and binders in scores of bookcases around the walls.

Marissa waited until the recorder walked around to the other side of the desk. A large, red leather chair stood between her and the desk, but when she began to move toward it, Mr. Harper pulled a smaller, straight-backed chair to his right. "Come and sit here, Miss Rosefield," he said. "Marissa? Is that it?"

The minute she had realized there were three people in this office working for Washington D.C., she had started to feel uncomfortable. "Yes, sir."

"Call me Blair," he said easily, as though he had asked a thousand people to call him by his first name. He leaned forward in his chair. "I'm glad to meet you."

When Marissa sat down, she crossed her ankles and immediately lost control of her shoe. But she didn't move. She waited while he rearranged some papers on his desk.

"We've been aware of your family for quite some time," Blair Harper said. "And we offer condolences for the death of your parents."

"Yes. Thank you." Marissa didn't know what to say. She had guessed that people from New York and Washington D.C.

would have been acquainted with the family because they owned the one farm the National Parks Association had wanted for the purpose of finishing out the park. Although government representatives had come to talk to Bradley Rosefield several times in the past, without success, Marissa had never been face to face with one of them. And here she was, in the government office with the county recorder, who was evidently involved somehow. She swallowed and tried to get her foot back into her shoe.

"Harriet tells me you don't have your papers," Blair said.

"Yes," Marissa said. "We'd like to know if we can get copies."

While he treated her politely, Blair Harper seemed to be very smooth. That he was bright beyond what Marissa had ever known in the Springdale population went without saying. He looked at her with an expression in his eyes that she had never seen before.

"Tell me about yourself," he said. "How old are you?"

Marissa's throat tightened. "I'll be nineteen." For some reason, the words felt thick on her tongue. She was sure that if she were to request title to the property, she ought to be as old as possible, though she had only recently turned eighteen.

"And your family?"

"My four brothers and I live on the farm."

"I have been to the park." Blair still sat upright in the chair not a foot from her. "I have seen the orchard, and the fields at the foot of the Watchman. It's a lovely place to grow up."

"Yes," Marissa said, then waited.

Finally Blair leaned back in his chair. "We can help you. But there are some difficulties."

She had expected some obstacle to raise its monstrous head. It seemed to happen any time her family had dealt with the government over licenses, taxes, and the like.

Blair stroked his smooth-shaven chin. "They have to be copied by hand."

"Yes, I understand," Marissa said.

"It will take a period of time. And require a periodic fee."

There it was. The expense. But Marissa and the boys had discussed that issue. The cantaloupes were ready for harvest now, and money would come in for those.

"I am not sure the records can be found right away," Blair went on. "You would probably need to check them. Are you willing to come back in a few days to make sure we extract the correct documents?"

Something about the county recorder unsettled her. Yet at the same time, she felt relieved. Now she knew—no matter how difficult or how long the process, it seemed they could get copies of the records. Of course she would have to come back in a few days, whether it was necessary or not.

"It's quite a drive," she said simply.

"I know that." Blair tipped his head as though examining her with microscopic eyes. "I'm sorry. But . . ."

For a moment there was absolute silence. Something in the room wavered with the light from the window. Marissa noticed a branch outside the glass that hit, hit, *whoosh,* hit, like the metal brush on a snare drum. She blinked, facing the light.

"It's the only way." He paused and smiled. "Do you have a telephone?"

She explained that the family sometimes got calls in Bertie Smith's store.

"So, an appointment will be necessary. Give your number to Bruzy on your way out, and I'll see you in a few days."

For a moment Marissa thought she was in the office with a doctor. But she had been to Dr. McIntyre in Hurricane only once, when Joey broke his arm. And that was several years ago. If government visits seemed as necessary as doctor visits, so be it. At least there was a solution she could present to her brothers.

When Blair rose suddenly from his chair to walk her to the door, she was surprised.

"Nice to meet you, Marissa Rosefield," he said.

Nine

Marissa waited outside the courthouse in the shade of a tree until Carter and Morgan came with the lumber in the truck to pick her up. When they arrived, they got out the soggy peanut butter sandwiches in the lunch bag, along with the apples and carrots.

"So, how did it go?" Carter finally asked her with his mouth full.

Crammed into the middle of the seat between her brothers, she wasn't sure how to tell them everything. "It's a long process," she said, hoping the knot in her stomach would be all right with a carrot or two. "They want me to come back."

"I knew it," Morgan said. "Everything always takes forever with the government."

"It was strange . . ." she began.

"Strange?" Morgan asked.

She hesitated. "It seemed they already know a lot about us."

Her brothers didn't respond to that statement. They finished their food while Carter kept driving. Then he broke the silence. "Ready to go to the dance rehearsal?"

Marissa felt the food sitting in her stomach like a rock. "Well, can you take me home? You don't need me. There are always more girls than boys."

"But you promised!" Morgan said. "Michael has the tractor getting fixed in Springdale. He was going to bring it to the church in time to meet us. Remember?"

She remembered. *Michael.* She tried to relax. All the way into Springdale while they drove through Hurricane and La Verkin, she kept as quiet and still as she could, feeling cramped and spent. But when they reached the church parking lot and saw the tractor, some airiness slipped into her limbs that felt like a fresh gasp of air blown into a rubber balloon.

Since the completion of the new hall in the little church in Springdale a few months before, the local ward had begun to hold more dances and parties. Coach Blanchard had spearheaded the construction project that added a room large enough to hold a small country band and most of the ward members.

With renewed energy, Marissa followed her brothers over the threshold of the new hall built into the side of the old church. But the moment they reached the recreation room, she knew her suspicions had been correct. More than two dozen girls—it might have been three dozen—sat around the edges of the echoing expanse with their feet on the rungs of the folding chairs, some of the girls rocking and looking disappointed at the prospects in light of the disproportionate gender.

When the dance instructor, Coach Kit Blanchard, saw the Rosefields, he brightened visibly. "Oh, good, we have some boys! We're so glad you're here." He came to them, his cheeks rosy. "Come now. We're almost ready to get in formation." He raised his arm. "We'll look at height. Girls on this side, boys opposite."

Marissa watched her brothers hesitate.

"Come, Michael," Kit called out. "You're tall! Why don't we put you . . ." He scanned the line of girls—as varied, as chatty, as colorful as a flock of birds. "Julie's the tallest one. Good, Julie! Carter . . . come. Sarah Williams. Patty Flanigan—Morgan."

That's how it happened. Suddenly. As though it was a moment in time as light as a maple leaf blowing from its branch into the river and floating downstream. The boys stood unaware, really, of what had just occurred. Michael, a couple of inches taller than anyone in the room, stepped forward to his fate. There was no time for what happened in that instant to register with any of them. Kit Blanchard had spoken. Sarah walked shyly up to Morgan, and Patty Flanigan—her red curls bobbing on her ears—jerked from her chair, practically dragging it along with her good-sized foot, and trounced to Carter's side.

There were others: Marie and Jake, and in the corner, Wade Keller and Corinne, looking pleased to be together. There were perhaps a dozen boys. But no boys for Marissa.

"There are too many girls," Kit announced as though he had just had a revelation, "So we'll have the girls pair up together. Good. Hilary with Jennifer. Barbara, take Sally." And so on, until everyone stood in the circle opposite someone.

Marissa stood opposite Maxine Riddle—just a little younger, just a little taller, and certainly a little rounder, with a mop of dishwater blond hair that kept falling in her face. She was wearing a skirt so long her shoes would tangle in it and pull it skitty wampus until she grabbed the elastic waist and pulled it up again.

"It's like this," Kit told them, glancing at his wife, who stood with a child in her arms. "Come here, Della," he said. Della put the little boy on the chair next to his older sister. "It's like this," Kit said, placing Della two feet in front of him. "We'll do it in two rows, and I want the rows facing each other like this."

In an energetic swoop, he flitted from one person to the other, turning each in the correct direction, handling each with a swift hand on the arm or back.

Marissa watched Morgan and Carter eyeing Julie. She was dressed in a red sundress over a brilliant white ruffled blouse. She wore her hair in a ponytail with a silver barrette on her long bangs. At Kit's pronouncement of her fate, she had sidled up to Michael, her long, graceful arms at her side, and her large blue eyes glancing upward, which direction had probably never been a possibility before in the presence of any of the ward boys. Both Morgan and Carter looked awkward and dumbfounded.

Marissa agreed in that moment that Julie was beautiful. She was elegant. And tall. She looked like the models in the Sears Catalog pages. But did Julie know how beautiful she was? Marissa guessed she did, since all of the other boys were staring at her. Now she was standing so close to Michael, there was hardly any light visible between them.

"Now! One-two, one-two." Kit wasted no time in showing them the steps they were to take—first apart, and then together in the dance position. Marissa watched Michael and Julie. As they faced each other, Julie reached out to him. They began to laugh because Julie did it backwards and had to correct herself. Michael kept smiling. They finally got it right. In the dance position, they stood and waited for Kit's direction.

Kit took Della in his arms and began barking all of the orders. "Girls, put your right foot forward. Boys, your left foot back. All right." He stopped for a moment. "The girl couples will have to decide which one of you wants to be the girl, which wants to be the boy, because the directions will be different."

Marissa said she would be the boy.

"Good, because I was in a dance at school, and all I can remember is how to be the girl," Maxine Riddle said, reaching back again for the elastic waist of her skirt and hiking it up a notch.

The dance practice lasted for an hour. Afterward, there was a confusion in Marissa's heart. She had no idea the feeling would last for the rest of her life. Because when the results of the practice had ended, when her own life had come to an end, and when she had rested on the couch in her daughter's home, knowing she was ready to leave the world she loved, while the beautiful only granddaughter she had ever known brought her warm lemon juice in a thermos cup, Marissa finally saw what that very moment—the moment when Kit had put Julie and Michael together—had meant for her and for all of them, for the direction of their lives.

Ten

"All night we listened to the pounding rain," Ellen told them. "When I walked out in the morning, the light that was coming up over the Watchman looked like ribbons rising. The world was alive with light. It smelled fresh and seemed calm. So I washed the sheets and blankets outdoors in the yard, scrubbing them with bars of lye soap and rinsing them out in a bucket of water from the river. I hadn't really washed the bedding since Michael was born. It had been six weeks. I hung them to dry on the clothesline your father put up for me—he used some of the wire left over from John Flanigan's lumber cable.

"Morgan took Carter and the baby with him down to the chickens. Carter liked to tuck Michael into the little rusted wagon we salvaged from the days Grandpa Rosefield raised your papa Bradley—when it was still Pocketsville, and we met in the little chapel before Papa helped build the big hall on the side of the building. They had a big argument as to whether or not they should build in back or on the side, and the side committee won, so they brought the lumber down on the cable already milled, and the men put it up in a couple of days, all working together. And that day of the flood of 1908, Papa left early to go down to La Verkin because they sold shingles down there for a nickel apiece.

"So the truck was sluggin' through the mud, the wheels suckin' it up, but Papa had faith God was going to let them get that roof on before it rained again. He said he could hear the heavens cheerin'. And we walked out in that yard that sloped to the chicken pen and the river with all kinds of faith it was going to be a good day, when we suddenly heard that roar.

"If you ever heard the freight train huggin' the tracks like it would never let go, that's what it sounded like. Like them Greek gods described it—playin' bowlin' balls up there in heaven. If they was ever a game of bowlin' in heaven, it was that day. And I thought it was going to rain again. But when I listened to it with both ears cocked, I could hear it was rushing tumult through the red walls, clattering and screeching like a passel of noisy trucks. But I knew it wasn't trucks, because the road went only to Sinewava. And if it was trucks they would have to be phantom trucks grinding imaginary brakes bearing down on imaginary wheels.

"So after I put the sheets up on the line, I went back into the house to fetch the blankets, and when I dragged the covers out onto the yard, I could see what was happening up the river. A huge heap of tree trunks and twigs interlaced with rocks and boards from sheds built upriver—a huge pile of debris—was on the brink of comin' toward the chicken pen, and there was the kids in the chicken yard. Morgan was still takin' big handfuls of grain and spreadin' it out on the bank. I wondered if he was deaf, or why he looked oblivious, just puttin' out handfuls of grain and not hearin' the sound as deafening as any sound I have ever heard. And Carter was sitting on the bank by the little red wagon, throwing rocks into the river. I was terrified. There was no time. The boys looked up, and that wall of water and wood came rushin' toward them and scooped up the chickens, the grain on the ground, the roost—and everything that went with it. Including my sons. All three of them. Morgan, standing surprised, his eyes wide, and a look on his face I will never forget, before that water crashed into him, and he raised his arms and screamed. And Carter, sitting on that bank, trying to clutch at the little red wagon with the baby Michael in it, when the river churned around him and carried him with the wagon into the black mass so quickly I could not see him in the melee. I let go of my tears and my screams that echoed down the canyon walls like the sound of banshees. Still dragging one of the blankets, I ran, praying, not paying any attention to where I was going, but running and crying and bellowing, 'Hang onto the bushes by the bank. Hang onto the bushes by the bank!'

"When I reached the edge of the water, I reeled. But when I saw the investment of seven years of childbearing and childrearing swirling in a tossing slough of sticks and logs and mess, I bounded in, not knowing what would happen to me. It was providence that I still carried the blanket, for I threw it in Morgan's direction, and when he clutched it, I drew him to higher ground. Carter was clinging to a mesquite bush with every ounce of strength he could muster, and when six-year-old Morgan was safe, I threw the same blanket into the charging morass and pulled Carter out. The wagon with baby Michael was bobbing downstream, so I ran after it, howling and shrieking.

"It was all I could do to keep the wagon in my sight. It was being pushed and shoved downriver by the debris. I ran. I ran, and it was a miracle I kept my feet going across the uneven ground, past the rocks, past the trees and the bushes that tore my clothing with their thorns and briers. And I prayed, 'Let me keep that wagon in my sight!' And there was a miracle.

"When I came around a bent pine tree, I saw that the river had pushed the wagon into a circle of high rocks, where it bobbed and bobbed and tossed like a cork on the ocean. So if I could climb the rock into the small space below I could reach it. I tore my skirts away. They were ruined. I climbed across the rocks into the small whirlpool, thanking God, praying all the time that once I got into the little cave, I could get out.

"But when I finally saw the wagon, it was empty. Oh, my heart! No! Oh, no."

At this point, Ellen was quiet, taking a moment to pause in this most terrible story.

"The boys were running after me and would not stop, as much as I gestured and screamed to them to go back. I was terrified.

"I knew I no longer needed to climb the rocks down to get the wagon, but I would find Michael if heaven would cooperate with me. It would have to be a miracle now, but I knew God would help me. I knew He would. Climbing out of those rocks, I had a calm and peaceful feeling that God would help me find him.

"Even when I ran down the river, crying out and praying with every ounce of energy in my body, I knew. And so I ran. I ran and looked for the bundle, looked for anything I could find floating, and there was another miracle, the one I was crying for. Locked up in a brace of branches beside the bank was the baby, naked as the day he was born, lying head up in the brown water, with a coil of rocks, chips of wood, and slender twigs swirling around him.

"That was you, Michael." Ellen looked at him with a level gaze. "We almost lost you, dear son of our lives. We did. We almost lost you. But I know God delivered you to me for a special purpose." She stopped in this part of the story. "And you were blowing bubbles then, too, dear Michael. Remember when you were a child and you blew out of your lips, bubbles and bubbles? It was a habit from that day, Son. You blew for your life. And we gave you a whistle, and a horn, and finally, when we could afford it, a saxophone. And finally a bassoon."

Everyone loved the story. But even if Michael loved it most of all, he was shy about hearing Ellen tell it with such a tribute. He smiled. But he always wanted to get to the next story—the one about the government workers coming in to build the road in the rocks, digging the tunnels and setting up the Wylie camp in 1917. The tale about Mr. Wylie and his bride, who swept out the tents every morning with a broom.

Eleven

On the way out of the church at the end of the dance practice, the teasing was merciless. Marissa expected it.

"Well, Marissa, are you going to ask Maxine Riddle for a date? Or is she too much of a riddle for ya?" Carter guffawed.

"Don't you know Maxine goes back to Isaac Riddle, one of the original missionaries who came down from Salt Lake City to teach the Indian school?" Morgan asked dryly, as though that should redeem Maxine Riddle and quiet Carter's irreverence.

"Well, I didn't know that," Carter said. "But I knew Patty Flanigan's grandfather is the fellow who built the first cable to haul the lumber."

"So are you going to take her to the top of the mountain to show her what she doesn't know?" Morgan asked.

Carter had a laugh like a railroad steam engine—"Huh-huh-huh."

When they reached the parking lot, the boys argued about who would drive the slow tractor home. Since everyone was tired, they decided to cram four into the front seat of the truck and come back after the tractor tomorrow. Michael said he'd drive the truck. With three big people in the front seat, Marissa sat partly on Morgan's lap and pressed herself against the window. Some obtrusive knot still seemed to be stuck in her throat. Some powerful thread of nervous tension crowded the air with unspoken words.

She felt a palpable essence alive in the truck—Michael's joy. He was dancing his fingers on the steering wheel as he sometimes did when he was practicing one of his musical numbers on the bassoon, in perfect time. He was oblivious to the others, not joining in the conversation. And the other boys must have felt too much anger, jealousy, and perhaps too much pain to bring up the obvious. How did Marissa feel? She did not know for sure. She was happy for Michael. She knew he had enjoyed himself. And she knew all of them would be going to the next dance practice, and attempt to become experts for the performance at the Gold and Green Ball. But deep inside of her somewhere there was a dark, thorny place that tore at her heart. She hugged the window, but she felt Michael's presence on the other side of Carter, and she fought back the tears of her guilt and her yearning to sit in the middle spot close to the brother she loved.

Someone—probably Bruzy—at the county recorder's office had called Bertie Smith on the telephone at the Springdale store and left a message that Marissa was requested to come to St. George next Tuesday. Morgan brought the handwritten note home and handed it to Marissa with a penetrating look of anxiety.

"Bertie Smith said the county people just had some more questions they want to ask you," he whispered.

Marissa was scouring the frying pan where the potatoes had left it black, and coarse as sandpaper. "This soon?" She looked up.

"Yes," Morgan said. "They want you to go back on Tuesday."

Carter still had a mouthful of wheat toast. "We gonna get copies of the papers tellin' us we own this property?" he said through his stuffed cheeks.

"I think so." Marissa dried her hands and reached for the written message with the tips of her fingers. It read, *Missa: Co. R's off. Re: Rosevill prop. More queschuns. 9:00 a.m. Tuesday.*

Bertie Smith was the most affable grocer and postal clerk in all of Washington County, but it was well known that he couldn't spell.

Morgan made a point of saving their trip to Intermountain Farmers for Tuesday morning so they could take Marissa in.

On Sunday, she said hello to Maxine Riddle, who seemed to be in a stalking mood, clinging to her female dance partner with a volley of questions and comments Marissa mostly ignored her while she watched Julie sidle up to Michael with a brilliant smile. Marissa could not hear what the couple said to each other, but Julie was using her hands to make a great point, and Michael was smiling. Marissa launched a dart of shame against the knot tying itself in her stomach.

On Tuesday morning, Morgan took so long milking the cow that he did not eat breakfast. Finally, hurrying inside the house, banging the screen door, he huffed, "Let's go."

All the way into St. George in the truck, Marissa kept looking at herself in the little mirror on the back of the sun visor. She had washed her hair and it seemed silkier than usual, the brown curls framing her high cheekbones. "I could be an Indian," she thought to herself, gazing at her almond eyes as black as onyx. But she was a pale face—there was no question about that. Her cheeks were white against the bright sheen of her hair. Michael had always told her she won the Most Beautiful prize from the Rosefield gene pools. "You got Grandma and Mom's good looks." He would grin at himself. "I don't look like anybody."

Morgan was slow getting his chores done and the truck going. When he finally dropped Marissa off at the courthouse, she told him to check with Mrs. Montgomery at the front desk when he came back to pick her up. She was not sure how long it would take if she had to wait somewhere while they did the copying.

Mrs. Montgomery smiled at her today and nodded toward the document room. At that moment Tessie came out of her boss's office carrying a stack of books and records two feet high.

"He's waiting for you." Tessie tipped her head toward the door, her eyes flashing as she peered over the stack. Piled on top of Tessie's head were the thick black braids Marissa had seen last time hanging over the girl's shoulders.

The door to the front office was closed, but Marissa did not have to knock. Blair opened it himself and stood fully visible, his hat in his hand. "Ready to go?" he asked.

Surprised, Marissa did not answer him.

"Didn't she tell you?" he asked. "Bruzy was supposed to tell you I needed a tour of the property, and to ask you if it was all right to take your time until this afternoon."

Marissa felt her face turn red.

"Well, is it all right? Did you have anything?" Blair turned to lock the door with a key.

"Uh . . . yes. I mean, I don't have anything."

"Well, let's take my car." Which was a foregone conclusion, as Morgan had left Marissa behind.

Blair shut his overcoat at the lapels over his blue shirt. He wore heavy boots and carried a black briefcase. When he looked at her and down to her skirt and black patent-leather shoes, he said, "We'll have to take you home to get on something we can walk in." He seemed in a hurry, as though he had waited twenty minutes already, and it irritated him.

Bruzy appeared from filing somewhere in the back just as Blair brushed past Marissa to the front desk. When he saw his secretary, he scowled. "You didn't give her heads up on the tour," he half snarled.

Bruzy's look was a strange mixture of embarrassment and anger. "Sorry," she said in a sharp tone.

"I'll probably be back before you go." He said it between his teeth, as though he were angry with Bruzy and would not glance at her piercing eyes.

Marissa felt a breeze when he rushed by her. His coat brushed her arm.

He paused. "Ready?"

"All right," she said, still confused. But she turned around and followed him.

Blair did not take much of an interest in giving instructions to Mrs. Montgomery. So Marissa tried. "If my brother comes here to pick me up," Marissa told her as Blair briskly walked out to the back door, "please tell him what happened."

"All right," Mrs. Montgomery said, watching the county recorder's quick exit with what looked like surprise.

"I have some errands first," Blair said when they reached the car in the dusty parking lot. He opened the door to the black Ford. "I was hoping you'd be here early."

"I'm sorry. My brother was late."

"Not a problem bigger than we can handle."

Marissa sat in the passenger seat and waited while he went into two or three offices in St. George to confer with somebody—he did not fill her in on any of the details.

"Since we're running late, we'll eat here in St. George before we go out to Zion National Park. Do you have a preference?" he said.

It was a crazy request. She had never eaten at a restaurant in St. George. Or anywhere else, for that matter. Oh, maybe one time, when Papa took her mother into the clinic to discover the diagnosis. Dr. McIntyre said he believed the lump below her hair was a tumor of some kind. Had she ever fallen and hit her head in that spot? Had she been forgetful? Had she been angry? They had gone to a Chinese restaurant and ordered noodles with vegetables, from a Mr. Louis Foy, who also ran a Chinese laundry on the tiny main street a couple of blocks from Brigham Young's mansion on 200 West and 100 North. President Young had been dead now for fifty years. When they drove past his house, they saw some of the Church people bent over in the grapevines, harvesting grapes. Others were picking pomegranates off the trees in the orchard.

"I don't know the eating places that well," Marissa said.

"Well, never mind," Blair said. "I'll take you to the coffee shop. They serve good sandwiches."

It was a tiny shack south of town on the road at the foot of the mountain that crossed St. George Boulevard. On their way straight west to the cliff, Marissa regarded the huge black foothill that loomed over them as though it were St. George's thumb sprawled on the land around them with a clutch as firm and binding as the ancient George Albert Smith himself, whose name had settled over the area.

The waitress in the shop was a heavy, matronly woman with a hairnet on a bun at the back of her neck. "Blair! Glad to see you. And this is . . ." She looked hard at Marissa as if she were naked. "You know this scoundrel of a man?" The woman chuckled.

"Not yet. She doesn't know me. And let's hope she never will." Blair tossed his head back and gave a cackle that surprised Marissa.

"So what'll it be?" the waitress asked.

"Send us some of your open-faced turkey to that booth over there," he said. He did not ask Marissa what she wanted, or whether or not she would eat open-faced turkey. Or whether or not—sparing the vision of a turkey with an open face—she could even guess what it was.

"All right. I have some questions," he said after they had scooted into the booth and sat over the oilcloth-covered table. "How come no man has ever scooped you up? Or has he?"

Marissa was speechless.

"All right. You're only eighteen years old. That should be the answer. Haven't you ever been in love?"

She almost choked on her answer. "Not really."

"So! Don't they have dashing young suitors in the hidden vales of Zion National Park?"

Marissa thought she ought to join in with the conversation. She was sitting as far back against the high-backed bench as she could. She knew Blair was joshing with her. She should stop being nervous, relax, and at least act like a human being. "A few," she offered. "It might be hidden, but there's enough that goes on, like in anybody else's town." When she said it, she tried to smile. "My brothers do their share of courting."

"Ha! I didn't think the natives of Zion National Park were as reserved as the rest of the people around St. George."

What did he mean by that? "We have our standards."

"Standards, blah. All of the people around here are tighter than drums. What do you do for fun?"

"We play checkers. We take hikes. We play music."

"You're one of those, eh? A checkers player." Blair sat back in his chair and pulled a big plaid handkerchief out of his pocket. His eyes were bright from the light in the window, and his gaze was penetrating. "You're too good lookin' to sit around playing checkers, Miss Marissa Rosefield." He paused to wipe his lips. "I'll bet you don't even know what it is to have a good time."

She wasn't sure she should say thank you to his compliment that she was good looking, or to probe further into his definition of "a good time."

"Do you drink?" he asked.

"No." She knew the answer to that one.

"You're like the rest of 'em, eh? Well, you all don't know what you're missing."

A welcome interruption was the appearance of two plates balanced on the arms of the waitress and cook, both slabs of white bread buried under slices of turkey and swimming in gravy. Small dollops of cranberry sat on the side next to a sprig of parsley.

"So where did you get this beauty?" the waitress asked.

"She's one of the party that owns that piece of property the government needs to complete the entrance to the Zion National Park."

"Ain't they got that solved yet?" the woman asked. "Mr. Albright was in here not too long ago, and I thought I heard him say the old man and his wife died, and they was going to give that piece over to the park for a museum."

Blair sat back and began to take his arms out of his trench coat. "Not yet." When he said it, he stared at Marissa as though he could not miss a moment of whatever was happening in her face. "We'll see."

She looked at her plate and thought that "turkey on a shingle" or "open-faced turkey" was a lot of food. She tried to register the fact that she was sitting in a St. George café with the county recorder, an outsider who suggested she had never known what it was to "have a good time." But he had told her she was beautiful. She couldn't think of anyone in her life who had told her those words—other than Michael—so they were still crawling around in her brain, stalking her thoughts.

She stared at her food and thought of how the only outsiders she had ever known to cross paths with the locals seemed to be committed to a way of life so different from theirs. They seemed to have no interest in building a bridge of understanding with her culture. They did not look at the settlers as thoughtful, breathing human beings. They praised the park, but seemed to dismiss the inhabitants.

In turn, Papa had always tried to gain the outsiders' favor. He always told enthusiastic stories about the "government people" who came through the park issuing expressions of such admiration as "I've never seen anything like this before," or "I never could have imagined . . ."

When Marissa was seven years old, Papa burst in from the barn one morning, interrupting the pancake breakfast with news that their old bishop David Hirschi's son Claud was on his way that day with a Frederick Fisher, a Methodist minister from Ogden. He heard from Bishop Hirschi that he ought to find out what was in this place. He had been on a touring trip with Jim Owen, the man who had killed so many cougars, bobcats, and coyotes that he had become famous. Owen had evidently told him remarkable stories of the spirits of dead Indians haunting the river walls. Claud wanted Morgan to go with them.

Morgan had leaped up from the table so fast he about tipped the remaining breakfast on his lap.

"Can I go too?" Carter asked.

But Papa said, "No. Claud wanted to know if Morgan could come."

And Morgan reported that the afternoon with the preacher was one of the most exciting of his life. They had begun a naming game. First they hiked past the three imposing peaks on the left, which Claud said looked like Abraham, Isaac, and Jacob. Doctor Frederick Fisher said, "The three patriarchs, eh?"

"Yes!" Claud shouted. "We'll call 'em the Three Patriarchs."

When Claud and Morgan decided the rest of the mountains ought to have names as well, they began in earnest to chase here and there with a dozen monikers that are lost to history. The park was called Mukuntuweap then. It was September 1916. It had been established as Mukuntuweap, but Fisher heard the young men call it "Zion." They reviewed the story of how Isaac Behunin called it Zion, and Brigham Young said, "This isn't Zion," so the inhabitants called it "Not Zion." Perhaps Frederick Fisher forgot how to spell Mukuntuweap, because he told the assistant director of the U.S. National Park Service, Chairman Albright, to approach the authorities to change the name to Zion.

At the loop in the river, the boys stopped at the pillars of rock looming above them on the curve. When he caught up to them, Mr. Fisher asked them why they had stopped.

"We're waiting for the organist to play the Great Organ," Claud told him.

When they reached the massive flat-topped peak in the center, Claud shouted, "Oh, Doctor, look quick. What is that?"

Mr. Fisher was in the game by now. Overwhelmed, he murmured, "Never have I seen such a sight before. It is by all odds America's masterpiece. Boys, I have looked for this mountain all my life but I never expected to find it in this world. This mountain is the Great White Throne."

After Morgan told his version of the story, Papa always embellished it with his extended tales. He kept track of Mr. Albright, who took Director Mather's place while he was ill for several years, went back to Washington D.C. and regaled his boss with glowing descriptions of the park. Papa loved telling how Mr. Mather thought Albright had been drunk when he saw the park. Mather put off visiting the park until 1918 when he was finally well enough to travel. When he finally did see the magnificent rocks, Mr. Mather was absolutely bowled over by the scene. He insisted it not be touched by commerce. When the road to Sinewava was completed in 1925, and the Utah Parks

Company wanted to build a hotel where the Wylie tent camp had been purchased in 1917, Mather said no. He conceded that a lodge that blended into the park might be acceptable.

"You're far away," a voice out of the distance said.

Marissa looked up. Blair was snapping his fingers in her face, or rather over the remainder of his turkey on a shingle.

"Where are you, girl?" he said. "You're lost in thought."

She raised her head and gave a laugh. "It happens to me. Sorry." She went after some of the turkey gravy with a crust. She wanted to ask him some questions, and now might be a good time. "Did you know the assistant director, Horace Albright?"

Blair narrowed his eyes and glared at her. "You know about Horace Albright?" It was obvious he hadn't expected her to know anything.

"He was the director of this park while Mr. Mather was ill."

Blair leaned back. "Aha! So you're not fully unaware of what has gone on here."

"We've been watching."

"Do you know they are about to bring in the big equipment to carve that road on the side of the rock?"

Marissa smiled. He became a person instead of a threat in that moment. "We've seen the trucks thunder past on the new road the convicts built."

"You live in the most amazing spot on the planet," Blair said.

Marissa leaned back and pushed her plate away. "That's why we're hanging on to it."

Comfortable in her overalls and boots, walking across the farm with Blair Harper was not as unpleasant as she thought it might be. As a matter of fact, he turned out to be good company.

"We own 360 acres, but there are only 14 that can be farmed," she told him.

Blair turned to her. "Well, we won't walk all 360 acres," he said lightly. "I just want a sense of what you have here."

Marissa took him to the southeast corner first. She paused for a moment. "What we have is . . . Zion." She looked at him out of the corner of her eye to see if he took her seriously. "And it wasn't easy for people to stay here with nothing to eat under the harsh sun and the threat of floods. Sometimes nothing but dandelion greens, watercress, and cactus jelly."

"Cactus jelly?" Blair grinned. "You ever eat it?"

"It's good. Made from yucca."

He stopped at a spiny, flaring plant that resembled huge pine needles. "Mrs. Montgomery told me the Mormons made tea out of this. She said the Indians showed somebody."

"Brigham tea."

"Mrs. Montgomery in our office adopted an Indian girl. You met Tessie, didn't you?"

Tessie was adopted by Mrs. Montgomery? Marissa'd had no idea.

"She was a wild girl. Her mother worked for the Dixie Cotton factory and left Tessie in a shack every day to fend for herself. Mrs. Montgomery brought her into her own family of ten, paid for her education, and made a secretary out of her." Blair gave a little laugh. "Not a great secretary. As I remember, she dropped papers all over the floor that first day we met."

Marissa looked at him. He was smiling, and the sun shone through his gold hair. They were taking the long way to the south, tracking through the brambles. "And this is where we believe my father climbed the Watchman to bury the box with the papers in it," she told Blair. Standing along the corner of their lot were tiny orange flags tacked to wires.

"The park surrounds you on three sides now. You knew that, didn't you, Marissa?"

She grinned. "I did."

"What are you going to do if you don't get the papers that say you own this piece, and the government performs some tricky deal—like eminent domain—and kicks you out?"

"This is the United States of America," Marissa said, as if that was the answer for everything.

"Ha! The United States of America is made up of human beings of all stripes—good ones and greedy ones. Careful ones and careless ones. A good president might appoint a sneaky officer. You're not assured of anything."

Marissa glanced at Blair. "They wouldn't take our farm away from us. This is America."

He was silent as they trekked back through the brambles she had negotiated only a few weeks ago with her brothers. "Just curious. The government's willing to pay a heap of money for this farm. What would you do if they made you sell it?"

As far as she was concerned, it wasn't going to happen. They had built enough buildings on the property to claim a fair presence, and no one could dispute that it had been theirs long before—just after Mr. Heaps and then Mr. Jolley had owned it. After a couple of minutes, Marissa finally said, almost inaudibly, "They haven't taken it from us yet."

When they reached the orchard, Blair stopped, looked around, and took a big breath. "I love trees. Get much fruit here?"

"Enough to make it worthwhile. All our trees were sprouted from seeds we sent for in catalogs."

"It's beautiful, Marissa." He smiled at her. The wisp of hair on his brow had fallen into his eyes. He looked at her and tipped his head. "What do you say we go into town and take in that new movie they're showing at that little theatre? You would go with me, wouldn't you?"

Marissa couldn't say she hadn't enjoyed the afternoon with him. Something about the farm glowed in the sun as it began to settle over the Three Patriarchs. Something about the fact that he would be driving off in his car in a few moments struck her with a small tug against her heart that felt like emptiness.

"No, I couldn't. But thank you anyway. I need to fix supper." She looked down at her boots, feeling suddenly shy when the focus shifted from the farm to her.

"Take a rain check on that?" Blair cocked his head.

She smiled. "Sure."

"I'll leave you to your cooking." He ambled off but stopped and gazed at her one more time. "I've really enjoyed visiting with you, Marissa. I had no idea what you were like, or what your people are like. I feel I've learned something here. Thank you for showing me around."

"You're welcome," she replied, for the lack of anything else to say.

Twelve

When things would go wrong, when Billie Poll's dog got mauled by a cougar up Oak Creek Canyon, or when the Calloway boys took their girlfriends up on the cable to a picnic and were killed by lightning, when the entire canyon seemed to be in mourning and Marissa was so affected by disaster that she wanted to stay home from school, her mother would talk to her about the "furniture of the mind."

"Where do you want to live, Marissa?" Ellen would say. "Most of where you live is in your mind."

It was best, she always said, not to know everything. She told her children, "You have one life to live here on earth, and sometimes terrible thoughts come into your life and become the kind of furniture you don't need there. And your mind gets cluttered with ugly things."

Marissa could not help remembering every pig they ever killed, every calf, or cottontail—even the wild animals. She could never ditch the images of Jim Owen coming into the canyon with his pack of hounds that chased the cougar up a tree. The hounds whined for what seemed like hours while Owen bagged the cat, which had been eating the saddles in the Rosefields' shed. Hearing the melee, the neighbors gathered at a distance to watch while Jim raised his rifle and shot the cougar. The bullet went right through the cat's eye, and the big animal jerked back and rolled out of the tree like a bag of stones.

When the boys heard the excitement, they ran. Michael was about thirteen years old then. He grabbed Marissa's hand so hard that she felt all the blood would leave her fingers. "Let's go see the cougar," he said. She was always ready to go with him. Holding tight to each other, they ran across the ditches, across the field of old melon vines, to the tree where the other children stood watching old Jim Owen reload his smoking gun.

Some of the cougar pelts ended up with Bird. Rumor said that many years ago, Jim Owen stayed with her somewhere in the canyon, and Marissa believed she finally knew where that was.

Once, the Beehive girls went for a compassionate-service project to Grafton to take fruit and bread to Bird in the home the Church made for her there. Marissa saw two or three furs that looked like cougar pelts nailed on the outside of Bird's shack. She believed they were probably Jim Owen's trophies.

There were things Marissa didn't know about Jim Owens and Bird. Ellen said, "It's all right not to know things. You are better off not hauling into your mind things like a greasy rug or an old, dusty bellows—furniture you'd be better off to discard."

Ellen told stories Marissa knew would probably last forever, like the time the ladies wanted to gather grapes from the other side of the river and weren't sure where to cross the carriage through the water. Ellen said that because of the treacherous ruts in the slough, the women prayed hard for the Lord to show them the way. When they opened their eyes, they saw two silver lines in the water as wide as the carriage. They drove right through those lines to the other side, and when they looked back, the silver lines were gone.

Miracles were okay to keep, Bradley told his children, adding that most of the time you had to make your own miracles. But he always agreed with Ellen, that you were the one who furnished your own mind.

Now, Marissa knew it was all right not to put thoughts about Michael and Julie in her mind. She believed with all her heart it was better not to know. She could see what happened on the dance floor. They laughed with each other and smiled together. When Michael's eyes twinkled, they almost disappeared in the crescent of his cheek, like the harvest moon disappears at the end of its cycle—just a sliver of a window into his soul.

Marissa dropped out of the dance practices when Maxine got a hankering for Wade Keller. And when those two got together, they also dropped out. Marissa didn't know what was happening between Maxine and Wade until months later when Maxine swelled up with Wade's baby, and he began coming to the house more often to beg Morgan for work—even when the truck was running fine. Wade was desperate for money because he and Maxine felt they ought to get married and set up housekeeping, and the best place they could find was in town with Mrs. Montgomery. The Montgomery family made a little place for them in their garage.

One thing Marissa knew was that Michael was not a Wade Keller. She wanted to be happy for him, so she rejoiced with them all at breakfast.

"I won't be able to take you to St. George today," Michael told her when she needed transportation for her continued trips to the offices of the county recorder. "I'm going up to see if I can get a job working on the Zion Tunnel in that camp they're building for the workers up there."

"I hear Doctor McIntyre was asked to settle up there at that camp when they get it going," Carter chimed in. "There's gonna be foreigners and miners, and all kinds of men come in there to work that tunnel."

It would be one of the most expensive roads ever built by the United States, everyone said. But the east and west sides of the park needed to be joined up, and that steep side of the mountain was the only place it could be done. There was one level spot in the middle where they hired a contractor to build good, sturdy rock buildings to accommodate all of the construction people. The entire canyon was affected by the big trucks carrying equipment and men to the site.

"Well, I can't take her," Morgan said. "I've got peaches to pick. I wish you'd learn to drive, Marissa. I can't figure why you have to go to the recorder's office so many times."

She didn't answer because she didn't know. The papers were slow in coming. But she thought that if someone taught her to drive, it would be a good idea for her to take herself, so she took notes on how Morgan stopped and started the truck, and she began to practice driving around the yard where the grass was cut short, and in the hen yard where the hens ran in front of her, squawking and trying to lift their fat bodies off the ground.

But Marissa wouldn't be ready to drive into St. George for several more months, though the county offices continued to ask her to come back because they had more questions. Or so Bruzy told Bertie when she left messages at the country store. It seemed the documents were never ready.

Blair sat at his desk, shuffling through papers beneath the lemony light in the high windows. He asked if Marissa knew about the Indian called Shunes, after whom they named the creek and the old town Shunesburg. She knew that when he sold his land he stayed on it, and years afterward insisted the settlers take care of him. She remembered Joey was afraid of him when he saw him by the river. Or was that old Pawgits? She couldn't remember.

Did she know why the park was called Zion? How many times had Bradley, and sometimes Michael, told her the story of Mr. Behunin, who had been a bodyguard to the Prophet Joseph Smith? "He helped build the temple in Kirtland and suffered the persecution in Missouri. He went west with Brigham Young, and in 1862 to the south country. When he saw the safety of the red hills for the first time, he exclaimed, 'These are the temples of God, built without the use of human hands. A man can worship God among these great cathedrals as well as any man-made church. This is Zion.'"

Acting on the 1906 bill that set aside national parks, President Roosevelt established Mukuntuweap in 1909. The name had disputed Indian translations all the way from "red dirt" to "straight canyon."

Blair leaned forward over some official-looking paper and mumbled, "Township 40 to South Range 10 from Salt Lake City." He paused and looked at Marissa again. "Do you know why they changed the name to Zion?"

Over the two weeks she traveled back and forth to the office with Morgan, she grew weary of such questions. But at least she had a chance to refresh her memory of the stories her father would tell over the dinner table. Sometimes he would move the dish of coleslaw and the platter of roast beef across the table, spread his elbows, and carve a map into the oilcloth. "There's Indian treasures all over the place," he would say. "Arrowheads, bones. There's treasures just in the stories the old people tell—about how brave Jacob Hamblin was to stand up to the natives."

Marissa remembered that story, always watching her father's piercing gaze as he tried to assimilate that bravery into his own character. His favorite story was about an Indian war in which a wounded native insisted that Jacob Hamblin give up his life to make reparation for the death of an Indian friend. Hamblin, who had not killed the Indian, tried to defend himself. Pleading innocence did not seem to work, so he recited all the ways he had been good to them. He had let them use some of his tools and taught them to plant grain. He had helped them irrigate. They agreed he had done all of this. So, the natives said they would accept 150 horses and cattle in exchange for his life. Still, Hamblin refused. Finally, they said they would let him go if he would let them stretch him over the hot coals of the fire as punishment. "Aren't you afraid?" the interpreter asked. "No," Hamblin told him. "You need never be afraid in the presence of your friends." And apparently he never was. The Indians finally accepted the payment of an ox.

When it was silent, Blair stood and walked to a bookcase behind his chair. "Have you ever heard of Zane Grey?"

Marissa hadn't.

"He was a fiction writer. Kept a six-shooter under his pillow." Blair pulled a book out of the stack. "He came to the canyon in the spring of 1907 to hunt mountain lions. Then he wrote about the trial of a cattle rustler."

Marissa politely took the book in her hands and looked at it. *The Heritage of the Desert.* "Hmm." She turned the pages. "Looks exciting—cowboys and cattle rustling." She had seen several articles in magazines about the West. "But cattle rustling isn't all there is to the West. There's another story to be told," she said. "About the hard-working pioneers."

Finally, on one of those days they were sure the records were ready, she came early. Navigating her way through the archway, she found Bruzy gone, and Blair's door open. When Marissa entered his office, she was surprised at the mess. He closed his door behind her. It looked as if he was in the process of tearing brown paper and rags from a shipment. There were two large paintings in frames standing in the clutter. Carefully, he peeled the last layer of brown paper from one of the pictures and set it in front of the bookcase. It was an amazing work of art. A deep blue sky embraced a shaft of light illuminating the red rocks she recognized as their own. She caught her breath.

"Do you like it?" he asked, watching her.

She was stunned at the beauty of the dark mountains, the red cliffs.

"Some arts council in Washington D.C. hired Thomas Moran in 1873 to paint the place. And nobody believed him." Blair ripped off the rest of the paper. "They thought it was a fantasy he thought up when he was drunk."

He smiled. "The other one's a Dellenbaugh. He painted this at the same time an article appeared in *Scribner's Magazine* in January 1904 about this place, calling it 'A New Valley of Wonders.' And his paintings were a hit in the 1904 World's Fair in St. Louis."

Marissa wasn't listening to him. She had never seen such amazing representations of the canyon she loved. For a moment she was speechless—as though the red monoliths of Zion had suddenly materialized into a miniature magnificence that now fit into a space as small as this room with walls.

"Come here," Blair said.

When she rose from the chair, she felt lightheaded. But she walked to him.

He reached for her hand. She did not know what happened to her heart in that moment. It may have been the amazing vision of the canyon in an art form that stunned her. But whatever had happened, Marissa gave him her hand. A shock went through her.

He closed his hand over her fingers. “Look at the strokes in this work. You will never see a more beautiful work of art,” he whispered, bringing her close. She drew near to the painting, not sure why the word “strokes” seemed to reverberate in some other way to her awareness. But when he put his arm around her and held her so close that her hair brushed his cheek, she recognized that the power overtaking her had happened only once before in her life—when she had rushed into Michael’s arms.

There was an awkward silence, until, not wanting to be impolite, Marissa drew a few inches away. But it was not far enough. Blair took her by the shoulders and faced her squarely. “Are you afraid?” he said.

She was trembling. When she began to speak, he drew her near the window. Clinging to her right arm, he stood over her and brought his mouth so close to hers that she could not breathe.

“It surprises me you have not known,” he whispered.

Known what? Marissa wondered. But she didn’t speak.

“You are the embodiment of everything I’ve found here.” He put his arms around her. “May I kiss Zion?”

He did not wait for an answer. His lips came over hers, and to her surprise she responded. She reached up and unleashed a hunger she had never suspected might have been hers.

Those weeks after the encounter in the office, Marissa walked in a daze. Nothing seemed real. While Morgan and Carter continued to harvest, Michael left each morning to work on the tunnel. He placed his tool belt and boots by the door to grab on his way out.

“You think you’re making money,” Carter sneered over his toast and jam.

"You can't support a family on that job," Morgan added, pouring cream on his oatmeal.

Support a family? Marissa stopped over the bread she was buttering for Michael's lunchbox. She turned from the sink to the table. While she had been in St. George, crazily sorting out what was happening to her, something had been going on here that rang with a different bell from anything she had heard before.

Morgan must have sensed her surprise. "Yeah, didn't you know, Sis? Michael and Julie are talking about getting married."

Marissa still had the table knife in her hand. When she turned, she reached back to lean on the sink counter for a moment. Michael was busy pressing his hardboiled eggs down on his plate with the tines of a fork and slathering the mash with butter. He was intent on getting the eggs right, something he always did with precision. But he was smiling. Joey was chewing behind his hand, trying to stifle a laugh.

"It's too soon. You only been goin' with her for two months." Carter's mouth was full of peach marmalade.

"It doesn't matter how long you go with someone if you know it's right," Morgan said.

Michael looked up at Marissa and smiled. He was eating. He asked Joey to please pass the salt.

"Oh, Michael, I didn't know!" Marissa heard herself saying. "How wonderful! Oh, when will it be?"

"We're not sure yet," he said. "I've got to get money together. I want to go to school in Indiana and study music, and I want to take Julie with me."

Music. Marissa felt her heart leap. She breathed in sharply. All of the boys were watching her. Joey wasn't touching his plate anymore.

It was a moment that could have brought some ghostly wraith of anger, jealousy, or loss into the room, but Marissa gathered herself together. She was surprised, but if the truth were to be known, she had been preparing for such a surprise ever since she saw Michael at the dance practice two months ago. She had been taught by a loving mother and father, and she had read over and over again Jesus' words to love one another. Not ecstasy, but the kind of love that lifts another human being, the kind of love that gives them the opportunity to be the best person they can be. Music. School in Indiana. Of course. It was Michael. It was his soul. It was his destiny. "Oh, Michael. Music! I'm so happy for you."

No one knew where the music had come from. But it had swelled out of Michael like the bubbles of a pure spring. He had taken to it—even as a baby. As all of them grew older, and as they spent their evenings sitting out on the newly cut grass, absorbing the freshness of all that surrounded them—the shimmering buds of trees, the sound of the river—they listened joyfully to the music of Michael's bassoon. Ellen told them that when she found baby Michael still alive and well, sitting up against a cradle of branches caught in a corner of the rocks on the Virgin River, blowing those bubbles, she had a thought that he would never stop blowing.

He had gone from blowing away the flood, to blowing through slots he tore in Indian grasses, and finally between just his lips with the sound of a trumpet. At a church picnic, he blew on the bandmaster's clarinet because it was a temptation, standing upright on a metal stand just ripe for a ten-year-old to try. Luckily, the band leader was the large-hearted Orson Taylor, who heard the sound from behind the bushes and said, "That boy is making that much music?" If Orson didn't really appreciate the boy's efforts, he certainly played them up with a genuine act of amazement.

Orson gave generous chances to children, to everyone he met. In his early life he had been a rascal, but when he turned his life around, it was a full 180 degrees. His transformation happened on a lark with his friend George Ayers, long ago when the men were excavating the road to Sinewava. The two mischievous boys sat together under the shade of a huge rock, smoking forbidden cigarettes, when they suddenly heard a cracking sound and knew the rock had come loose and was about to fall on them. Orson sprang to his feet and jumped out of the way, but the rock fell on George and crushed him to death. Orson was so shaken by this catastrophe, he made a commitment to his deceased friend and to the people around him to make his life mean something. He was a Primary teacher until the day he died. He taught Michael to play the clarinet, and then the saxophone.

Michael's eyes were still twinkling. "Orson Taylor thinks I can become a music teacher in a university."

Marissa turned back to the sandwich and put the knife down. Facing the sink, she felt darkness. So she turned back. There was no darkness in the room, and the whites of Michael's eyes were still bright. "Michael!" she said. But still she had not smiled. "You'll do it. I think you'll do whatever you want to do." *Including marry the most beautiful girl in the canyon,* she thought to herself. But she didn't say it. She must rejoice with Michael. He was nineteen, almost twenty, and he would know what he wanted in his life. If she lost him from this house, she would not lose him forever. He was her brother. She loved him in a way that perhaps she shouldn't, but she knew they had done nothing wrong. Whatever love there was, whatever pulse of feeling that passed between them all of these years, it was something they could hear in their music. It was something they could pass to each other in letters and over the telephone.

"I'm happy for you," she said to him. "If there's anything I can do to help, let me know."

The silence in the kitchen was startling. Something had settled down, ephemeral yet almost tangible, so like their music, breathlessly accompanied by the flute that played in the distance—the song of the pipe they had never been able to find.

"We will be here for a while longer." Michael returned to his eggs. When they were almost gone, he slapped his hand on the table and got up. "Well, I've got to be going."

"Careful not to run into a mountain lion," Carter said.

It was a joke. Years before, Michael had gone into the yard and been startled by a bevy of quail suddenly rising in the air from behind the blackberry bushes. He wondered if the dog had frightened them. Curious, he carefully tiptoed his way to the end of the garden, where he caught sight of a cougar with its mouth full of blood and feathers. Michael had often seen the carcasses of birds lying in the cabbages, but he had never looked into the eyes of a fierce animal tearing its prey apart. Michael told them that a fear had gripped him in that moment—something he had never known before. And it impressed him that this was symbolic of life. All creatures lived by destroying something else. He had rehearsed the philosophy with Papa that evening before he took the bassoon to the canyon wall. Bradley had smiled and said, "The survival of the fittest." *The fittest.* "Work at staying fit," Papa had said. And then he died falling from the Watchman.

"Dr. McIntyre already took his practice up there." Michael pushed his arms through the sleeves of his parka.

"It's that dangerous?" Carter asked.

"I don't know. And his nurse—you know, the one with the herbs." Michael turned to look at his brothers and his sister standing with his lunch pail in her hand. "It's safe enough." He smiled. "The question is, how are *you* going to do without me?"

Joey pulled back in his chair and laughed. Carter threw his napkin at Michael. Marissa handed him the lunch pail. "We won't like it, but we might live." She laughed.

"I'll miss you!" Michael's eyes were so blue, Marissa thought she could see the reflection of the sky in them. But there was no sky. Just the dark beams of the house under the roof, the bright windows, and the light that shimmered through the curtains Ellen had made.

"All right," Marissa said when he opened the door. "Get on with you!"

Thirteen

The only way Marissa could get to St. George was with Morgan or Carter when they had to take produce to the markets, replace a tool, or purchase oil. Or repair a tire for the truck. If the truck would not move, Wade was still available to tinker with the motor. Carter swore he was going to learn what Wade knew so he could rescue the motor in its times of trouble. But it never happened.

"Wade is getting a little testy," Carter complained. "I think he wants more money. Says he wants to marry Maxine Riddle, and he needs a little more for the hours he spends keeping the truck running."

Morgan was always nervous about the truck. Because the bathroom was so small, he often shaved in front of the mirror above the desk in the living room. He didn't want to pay Wade any more. That was clear. "We pay him enough," Morgan said, scraping the razor across his neck.

"Well, you might not have a mechanic then," Carter sneered. "Of course, that's none of my business."

"He keeps taking that trail over to the Watchman," Joey piped up.

"Wade does?" Carter asked.

Marissa was taking the pan of hot water off the stove to wash the dishes. "He does?"

Joey turned to her. "Yes. That's where they put the flags and marked off where our property ends and the park land begins."

All of them ran into him once before, Marissa remembered. "How do you know, Joey?" she asked.

There was silence except for the scrape of Morgan's razor against his cheek.

"Joey, are you still going to the cliffs to see if you can find Papa's box?" Marissa asked uneasily.

It was an October evening, and the cold whistled down the canyon walls and rattled the leaves before it came into the house. Joey huddled in Papa's old chair by the window, and he drew up the quilt cover as though he would hide behind it.

Marissa's question wasn't accusatory. She simply wanted to know. "It's all right to keep trying, but . . ."

"You don't believe it's really there, do you, Marissa?" Joey said. He was growing, and the legs of his overalls reached the middle of his calf. There wasn't enough money to buy new shoes. Marissa noticed the holes in his socks.

"But maybe not the best use of your time. You have studies," Marissa said.

Joey was fourteen. He would be tall. His ash blond hair, in need of a suitable haircut, looked chopped and blown. Since Papa died, Joey had withdrawn into himself, it seemed. Yet there was anger in him that erupted at the most unpredictable times. "Well, you're supposed to be getting those papers," he said now to Marissa. "And it never seems to happen. What if we never do get them? Those government men—they know Wade. He talks to them. They are hot on our tails to get hold of this land, and if we can't prove nothin', they will take it from us."

Marissa knew Joey went out into the fields after supper with Rumbo. But she had never asked where he went. Or if she asked, he always said he was just taking the dog for a walk.

"Who is that Blair Harper fellow, anyway?" Carter asked. He was cutting holes in one of Papa's belts to make it smaller so he could use it. He stopped pounding on the awl and looked up as if waiting for an answer.

"He is the county recorder," Marissa said. "You knew that."

"Well, are you sure?" Carter tipped his head in a question. "'Cause he sure don't come across with any papers that seem like he knows any official business. How often you been over there, anyway?"

Marissa held the edges of the dishpan and leaned over it. She knew what her brothers would think if they were to know—if anyone were to know—what happened in the office behind closed doors. What would Bishop Robinson think? What would Joey say? What would anyone—Bruzy, Tessie, Mrs. Montgomery—say if they knew what happened when she rushed into the courthouse, through the front desks, and into the bright room with the high windows behind the closed door? They did not know he was no longer Mr. Harper to her, but Blair—that she flew into his arms and stayed there for untold moments, absorbing the freshness of his shaving lotion, feeling the waves of delight in her limbs as he embraced her and kissed her neck, her ears, her hair. If they left for lunch in the city, she smoothed her clothes and reapplied her lipstick. On the way down, she watched Mrs. Montgomery's eyes closely, because she believed the woman had a sixth sense that something more than transactions passed back and forth in the corner room. And sometimes it was Bruzy who pounded the door when it was locked and called out, "I know you're in there," and ended with, "Crap," before she left them alone.

"We'll make it official at Christmastime," Blair told Marissa. "Do you mind if we get married here, in the courthouse?"

She pulled back to look at his face. He was beautiful to her. The dark eyebrows over the golden hazel eyes. She loved his face—the strong chin. She often held his cheeks with the palms of her hands. The courthouse was not the place she had dreamed about getting married. But her dreams had flown with the death of her mother, and then her father. What would they say if they knew she was going to marry outside of the temple? They would be chagrined. But the courthouse was legal, wasn't it? And she was in love. "Anywhere, Blair."

"I don't want anyone to know," he whispered. "It could be found . . . unprofessional."

He said it at that moment because they heard rustling at the door, and he tipped his head to the sound.

"Who is it?" Marissa asked, thinking it sounded a little bit like Rumbo.

"Bruzy," Blair whispered. He mentioned once that she and her brother had gone with him from New York to Washington D.C., where they had been assigned to work here. "She gets close to my door when she's uh . . . filing." But seeing Marissa's penetrating gaze, he admitted, "I'm afraid she guesses . . . and she believes . . . she's being protective of me."

Even though the brushing noise stopped, it was always a few minutes before Marissa could focus on the maps and documents spread out before them. Soon, Blair reached for her hand. Then their feet came together under the table. The light from the high stained-glass windows fell on the desk in patterns of yellow, red, and blue. The leaves outside the window spelled joy in the autumn sky. Often, the light was falling in the afternoon when it was time for Morgan and Carter to pick her up—always in the truck, as they decided not to spend money fixing the Chevrolet.

On the next trip, she asked Carter if she could take the truck by herself.

"Do you feel you do a good enough job that you can get all the way to St. George?"

She had been practicing. "Yes."

When she drove into the parking lot, Bruzy was getting out of her car.

"Driving yourself now?" Bruzy said. "Well, it's about time!" She tossed her head in a dismissive manner, then strapped her big purse over her arm and locked the door of her model A Ford with a key. "Not so hard for a woman, right?"

Marissa tried to smile. She wondered what Bruzy was really thinking behind those green eyes. Marissa thought she detected some hatred that seemed almost material.

"You certainly have been persistent coming out here to get those papers," Bruzy almost snarled. "You are crazy thinking you are going to get those papers any time soon. You have no idea how slow things work around here."

Marissa was not sure of the tone in her voice, although she was certain of the content of her message.

"Mr. Harper has no intention of making it easy for you." Bruzy laughed. "You're crazy to keep coming back. If I was you I'd tell him to bug off and call when they are done."

Marissa felt the color rise in her face. "I've tried . . ."

"Ha! Not hard enough," Bruzy growled.

What is she talking about? Marissa wondered.

"You gonna drive that truck by yourself every day now?" Bruzy asked.

"Probably, if the boys don't need it. They're harvesting right now," Marissa managed to say. She was guarded in Bruzy's presence. The woman seemed predatory. She moved with a gait that seemed suggestive, and she tossed her blond curls as though she knew a secret. It bothered Marissa. But she listened to Blair, who said, "We live our own lives. We're not required to include everyone."

Soon Christmas seemed too far away, and Blair paid handsomely for the judge in the offices of the courthouse to seal their love with a quiet legal ceremony to take place on November 3rd. Marissa would wear her white lawn dress with the straw hat. She could tie the hat with new ribbons from the haberdasher on St. George Boulevard. It would not matter, because the only one to see them would be the judge and the judge's secretary, who would serve as witness. Blair did not want Mrs. Montgomery, Bruzy, or Tessie to suspect anything.

Sometimes Marissa wanted to tell her brothers what was happening. As she drove back and forth in the canyon, she believed the colors of the land had intensified. The strips of red across the basin looked rosier, the yellows mottled with dense green and black, the river alive with silver, speckled with dazzling sparks of sunlight that nearly blinded her.

Her trips were long, yet they seemed short to her. She was alive with feeling. This was what love felt like—to be in touch with the blue sky, the sage, the rabbits in the road, the water in the canals. Nothing mattered anymore except this love. It was such a glorious feeling, she would like to have shared it with her brothers.

Her brothers. While the world was brighter for her than ever, Marissa was still responsible for her brothers. Joey began to have trouble with his throat. His complaints began intermittently but were soon constant. He stayed home from church on Sunday. When she asked him to open his mouth, he could barely open it without emitting a cry of pain. In the back behind his tongue she saw that his tonsils were red and swollen. The only doctor for miles was Dr. McIntyre, who was taking care of the employees at the road camp where Michael was working.

Michael. For several weeks, when he was not around, she felt proud of herself for managing to bury some of her thoughts about him and Julie. Marissa saw Julie at church and felt constrained to be kind, to smile and say hello. But now, the thought of driving up to the camp and perhaps running into Michael startled Marissa with its power.

"You taking the truck today?" Carter asked her.

"I really ought to take Joey to see Dr. McIntyre," she replied. "His throat is swollen."

Joey was leaning over the breakfast table, his hands on his cheeks. "It'll go away."

"No, we ought to see what's going on," Marissa said.

"Well, we're still working on the cantaloupes," Carter said. "But one of these days we'll need to take them in."

"The truck's acting up," Morgan broke in. "Wade is coming this afternoon. Go ahead and take Joey up this morning. Isn't Tuesday usually the day you go to the recorder's office?"

It was.

"Take Joey up this morning. Wade should get it done this afternoon, and we'll take the cantaloupes tomorrow."

Driving up to the camp took a harrowing half hour. Marissa was immediately sorry she hadn't insisted that Morgan make this trip. He would've been savvy about the sound in the motor that seemed to interrupt and jerk. When the road rose against the steep hill to the tunnel project, she felt she could not breathe or the truck would tip and fall down into the slough. Ahead she saw the huge claws of the machines that dug up the hillside. The wasp-like drills. The clutches of men and boys, lifting logs, slipping on the red dirt, beating their dusty hats against their thighs.

"Watch out for that wheelbarrow," Joey said, practically leaning his entire head out the window, helping to navigate.

Finally at the camp, Marissa berated herself for having wanted so much to come here that she risked both of their lives. She knew she was coming, not only to take Joey to the doctor, but to see Michael. It was foolish, because she might not see him at all. But she was looking for him, and she hadn't seen him yet.

Joey got out of the truck and slammed the door. "Whew. We made it," he said. "I hope Wade can fix that knockin' in the motor. I thought we was gonna trip over the edge of those rocks and find ourselves in the river."

Marissa climbed out of the truck, and as soon as she put her feet in the red dirt, she remembered Papa calling it "devil's dust." It was almost impossible to scrape it off your shoes.

The doctor's quarters were behind the huge derricks and the digging machines parked in the yard. A series of well-constructed government buildings loomed against the mountain at the far side.

As they walked, Joey held his chin. "Dang. This thing hurts."

"We're almost there," Marissa assured him.

The road to the buildings was really the best way to get there, although the trucks driving through to the repair garage honked for Marissa and Joey to get out of the way.

They were within a hundred yards of the doctor's office when they heard a truck braking behind them. The driver's door opened and slammed shut.

"Marissa! Joey!"

Oh my! It was Michael. He'd stopped in the middle of the road and was running up to them. "What are you doing here?"

When Marissa turned around and saw him, her whole body abandoned any discipline she had ever mustered to forget him. Her heart beat fast as she took in his face, brown in the sunlight—his twinkling eyes, the grin. He took off his hat and waved it like a banner. "What's going on?"

"I'm going to see Dr. McIntyre," Joey said. "My throat's sore."

When he reached them, Michael stood a few feet away as he always had. But his eyes betrayed him. They were filled with longing. "I'm so glad to see you. Seems like forever I haven't been home—three weeks. They want me here. Just convenient. But how is everybody? I miss you!"

"We miss you too," Marissa said.

Was he going to embrace them? No, he'd better not. Marissa froze. She felt a staggering jolt in her body, as though she were electrified. She knew that was what she wanted, to hold Michael. The feelings had not gone away.

When he began to walk with them to the doctor, he beat his hat against the leg of his overalls, just as the others did. "Sorry about your tonsils," he said to Joey. "Heard you were having a hard time getting those papers," he said to Marissa.

"I think we can still find where they're buried," Joey said.

Michael laughed. "Well, whatever. It seems we're still sitting on the most wanted piece of land in the United States of America." He smiled at Marissa. "Are you still going to the recorder's office?"

Marissa held her tongue. Did he know something?

"I had a dream last night," Michael said. "I dreamed we were walking to the Watchman together. Joey was going to climb the mountain to find Papa's papers. And a great flurry of wings rose into the sky. Remember when the quail flew up because the cougar was in the corn?"

Marissa stopped walking and looked at Michael's face. "And so . . .?"

"Maybe my dream is trying to tell us something," he said.

But just then a huge *blat-blat* rang out against the hill. Another truck had pulled up behind Michael and wanted to get through.

"Hope I can see you later so we can talk," he said, backing away and waving to them.

Marissa watched him go.

Dr. McIntyre decided Joey ought to have his tonsils out at that moment. Neither Joey nor Marissa had suspected anything of the sort when they entered the infirmary and greeted their friend, Nurse Denette. They had to wait for half an hour. The doctor was treating a young man whose foot had been in the wrong place at the wrong time and broke under the teeth of a steam shovel. When the doctor was finally free, he sidled over to the faint light of a north window and used his flashlight to guide his sharp instrument as he probed to cut out Joey's swollen glands.

"There, that should do it." He waved the defunct pieces of Joey above the canister where Denette had put an inch of alcohol. "You want 'em for lunch?" he asked Joey.

Joey tried to make some kind of laugh happen in his bloody mouth. But Marissa was thinking of something else. Backing away from the lot crowded with trucks and cars and big machines, turning around at the road, and bumping and jerking along with the spitting engine all the way down the canyon, she could not stop thinking about Michael. She cared so much. She wanted the best for him. He was making life-long decisions. She wondered why she was thinking about him when tomorrow Morgan and Carter would take her in the truck with the cantaloupes to see Blair at the county recorder's office. She tried to think about Blair. She would be happy to see him.

That afternoon Joey was supposed to stay down flat and drink some herbal tea Denette had concocted for him. Marissa put sheets on the couch and plumped a pillow for him. "Stay here while I pluck the hens," she told him. She loved Joey too. Something in her heart swelled up with joy for her family. In just over a year and a half, she had become their mother.

She began with earnest to prepare all of the vegetables from the last harvest out of the garden. She cut up the pumpkin and boiled it to make pumpkin bread. Outside the kitchen window she saw Wade wheel himself on his dolly in and out from under the truck, fixing it while Carter and Morgan were out in the field piling up the melons.

Wade was an enigma. He was a talented mechanic and seemed intelligent. But he hadn't made any effort to take responsibility for his child that was growing in Maxine. *Doesn't he love the baby?* Marissa wondered. It was his own, a part of him more than anything else in his world was a part of him. Perhaps he didn't feel he had enough to give a family. He worked for only a few of the farmers in the canyon. He had tried to get a job at the camp, but found out the tunnel project had its own mechanic.

However, there was more he could give his own child and its mother, Marissa thought. He could give them attention and love. Also, she had seen him at church, but she knew he came so he could ask the bishop for grain from the storehouse. She thought if Wade paid his tithing he would be blessed. That had always been a miracle to Bradley Rosefield. When he paid his tithing he had never wanted for anything. And he taught his family to pay a tenth of every dime they made, or a tenth of what they harvested. They had done it for so long it was like breathing. Bradley used to say, "Just test it out." And he was always right. As long as they paid their tithing, they had never wanted for anything.

Sometimes Marissa watched Wade wheel himself out from under the truck. He didn't get up off his back, but stretched to reach the toolbox and rifle through the motley collection of bolts, screws, and screwdrivers, for another tool. Sometimes he rubbed his hair with his greasy hand before he grabbed a tool and wheeled himself back into the dark. He had been closemouthed about why he was talking to the government people about the flags they were posting, why he was hovering around the Watchman, why he was beating down the brambles in the path from the Watchman to the barnyard.

Marissa didn't want to leave the house for long in case Joey needed something, but she did walk out once when she saw Wade curled over on his dolly, reaching for a crowbar.

"Would you like something to drink?" she asked.

He mumbled something.

She didn't understand.

"I said sure, but you don't have it," Wade said in a stronger murmur.

Probably not, she thought.

He poked his head out from under the black maw of the truck's underbelly, his hair standing choppy on his head. He had a strange, taunting look in his eye. "You don't want your motor breakin' down in the middle of the road. Do you?"

No. Not really. "Well, we appreciate your help, Wade. We always do. Thank you for fixing it."

"Don't thank me 'less it works right," Wade said. "You ought to spend some money on that cranky Chevrolet. Or get a newer vehicle."

Marissa backed up inside the house and closed the screen door. That was the last time she spoke to him.

In the morning, Joey said he felt better, but he looked worse. He had black bruises all along his throat. And all he wanted to drink was Denette's herb tea. Marissa couldn't, in good faith, leave him.

"Oh, I'll be all right. You go on ahead to St. George," Joey told her in a scratchy voice.

But she knew she wouldn't be going with the boys and the cantaloupes.

“Do you want us to stop at the recorder’s office and see if they got them papers?” Carter asked her, slapping his gloves against his overalls.

“No,” she said. “I’ll go tomorrow.” Tomorrow would be all right. Blair would wonder what happened, but she would tell him then.

Fourteen

No one would believe what happened on the road to St. George if ever she spoke of it. When she first heard it, she could not believe it or accept it. She was boiling potatoes and scraping off the skins while Joey sat at the kitchen table, cleaning the rust off a harness. As dusk drew down over the canyon walls, Marissa expected Morgan and Carter to be back. She heard a vehicle approach the house, but the motor that stopped and the door that slammed sounded light for the truck. Through the window she saw Kit Blanchard climb out of his Model T and walk up to the door. Something in his face frightened her.

"Hello, Brother Blanchard." She tried to smile.

"Hello, Marissa." He did not smile.

"Will you come in?" There was an electricity in the air she could not explain.

"I came to tell you . . ." He paused and glanced inside the room at Joey. "Is your brother Joey all right? I heard he had his tonsils out yesterday."

Marissa knew he was not there to see Joey. "He's doing all right," she said quietly, waiting, feeling the heavy air press down.

"It's your brothers." Kit's voice came from a dry throat.

"Please, won't you come in?" She felt some oppressive terror that gave her a reason not to ask any other question.

He stepped up into the house while she held the screen door. "There's been an accident."

She knew it before he said it. The air sounded against her ears like the onslaught of a thousand wings of quail. She waited for more.

"An explosion," he said.

What happened next in Marissa's body was a rush of pain—as though she must keep her hand on the knob of the screen door or she would fall.

"I'm so sorry." Kit turned to face her. "Everything is gone. The truck . . . the cantaloupes . . ."

"My brothers . . ." she uttered without knowing she said it.

Joey had jumped from the table. "What's happened? What is it? What . . ."

Kit stood in the middle of the entry with his hat in both hands, his head bowed, as though the words must be uttered like prayer, or not at all. "We don't know what caused it yet."

No one in the room moved. There was a moment of such heavy silence, Marissa could hear the coals crackling in the stove, and the water boiling.

"Just before La Verkin. Going down that hill. It was perhaps too steep for the load. The officers do not know . . ." Kit Blanchard moved one hand from his hat to reach out to Marissa, but she backed up against the door and clung to it with every ounce of strength she had left.

"We are here for you, Marissa. My wife has already organized the Relief Society ladies."

Nothing he said made sense.

"How badly are they hurt?" Marissa finally got out.

But Kit lowered his head. "I'm afraid . . ."

"Not . . ."

"I am so sorry," Kit said, not looking up at all.

Marissa heard about the cantaloupes on the road, smashed and blown to pieces. But she could not imagine them. When Michael took her and Joey to the funeral home in their only remaining vehicle—the half-broken Chevrolet—there were still pieces of rind on the road. Joey hunkered by the back window, saying nothing. While Michael talked to the bishop at the funeral home, Joey stood behind them, his hands in his pockets. Marissa placed her fingers on the closed lid of the pine coffin the priesthood built to hold two bodies—or at least whatever remains had been found. The family would never know what had been pieced together by the mortician. As though still reaching for her brothers, hoping she could seep into the wood and stay with them for one last moment, Marissa pressed her fingers against the last place on earth they would ever know. When she finally backed away from the wooden casket, she tightened her fingers around her soggy handkerchief.

Michael came to her side. "Bishop Robinson asked if we wanted to play a duet for the funeral."

She held the handkerchief so tightly her hands had turned almost white.

"Could we do . . ." Michael hesitated as though mentally going through their repertoire. "Bach's chorale from the *St. Matthew Passion?"*

Marissa knew it and loved it. "O Sacred Head, Sore Wounded." She did not know how it would be—how hard it would be—to play with tears crowding her eyes. But she would do anything for Michael.

"Or '*Träumarei.*'"

She did not lift her face to him. She kept wringing her handkerchief, attempting to grasp the harsh reality—that whatever was left of Morgan and Carter would soon be lowered into the ground. How quickly the family had dissolved.

"Will you?" Michael said.

Marissa still had two brothers. And Michael was asking her to play a duet with him at the funeral. She felt his breath near her, as though he were fighting to catch the last air they could find to share together. She didn't speak but nodded without looking up.

She hadn't played for a while. The wood of the cello felt smooth beneath her fingers, as though it was flesh—as though it had missed her touch and would respond to her. When she removed it from the case, she took extra care to burnish the strings with resin. She was very much aware of Michael's mouth over the reed of his bassoon. She felt his mouth, and the press and moisture of his lips on the mouthpiece. When he and she began to rehearse, there seemed to be something in the canyon that may not have answered back with audible sound, but with a tangible peal that felt like an echo of spirit—something that reverberated back and forth between Steamboat Mountain and the Watchman. Sometimes the notes seemed to come easily, smoothly moving along the blood, beating with the heart, filling the large waves of space with pure yearning. This happened seldom, when everything in the universe followed a rhythm already decided on by the heavens. Marissa felt the harmony with Michael's instrument slowly change her, give her new life, like water. She had never felt so full, or so completely in tune.

That Friday before the funeral, the Relief Society sisters came with their husbands to the house to help finish the harvest. Sister Blanchard brought a peck of peaches and a chicken casserole. She brought her young daughters with her, who drew circles and squiggles in the Sears Catalog while Marissa and the other ladies peeled potatoes and made chicken pies to feed the workers when they were done. Even Wade Keller came to fuss with the old Chevrolet that sounded as though it would fall apart at any moment. He would try to get it in working order, he said. It was the only vehicle they had now. All these good people who surrounded them gave Marissa comfort. If they offered her a shoulder, or gave her a hug, she accepted it, burying her tears in their hair.

At night she lay awake, wondering if Blair would see the news, or wonder why she did not make it to the office that week. Finally, she took courage and called. Bruzy answered.

"Hello, is Blair there?"

"Hello. May I ask who is calling?"

"Marissa Rosefield."

"He's in a conference at the moment."

She did not want to interrupt anything. "Will you please tell him I am sorry, but the accident . . ."

"I'll have him call you," Bruzy said brusquely. She didn't ask about the accident. Blair did not call back.

Michael could not leave his job for any period of time. But he came to be with them for the viewing at the church. He and Julie stood beside the coffin and greeted the passersby warmly.

"It's all yours now," Bishop Robinson said. "It's up to you."

Michael smiled. His shoulders sagged, as though the responsibility had already begun to weigh him down.

In the service, Julie and her sisters sang "How Great Thou Art," and Bishop Robinson gave a tender eulogy that brought tears to many eyes. These were good young men. He remembered that Carter had always raised his hand in Sunday School class. His answers weren't always accurate, but he was full of hope that he could add something to what he must have seen as a humdrum repetition of what he had already heard. Several of his friends lowered their eyes into their palms and wept.

The chorale was flawless. Marissa knew the powers of heaven were guiding her hands when she clutched the cello between her knees. She played as she had never played before, and the sound rang in the room. Michael's eyes were so full of light, she looked to the windows for a moment to see if the sun came through the colored glass. The air vibrated with the harmony. She was not sure how the power of their music had materialized, but it had happened with grace and clarity.

When it was over and the three remaining Rosefields gravitated to the door, Julie held to Michael's elbow as she might hold to a metal pole in a bus that was rocking and threatened to overturn. Her father was smiling and gracious, herding the crowds as he did after every Sunday meeting. "We are so sorry about your brothers, Michael," Bishop Robinson said. "But happy to hear the news about your wedding at Christmastime."

Wedding at Christmastime? Michael? Marissa felt a stab of pain through her heart. This was the first she had heard of such an event. Michael had not told the family. She looked up at him. He was smiling. He took her wrist in his hand and held it. "I was going to tell you soon," he whispered.

In this moment, Bird, the old Indian, was going through the line, and she smiled at them. "You have wedding, I give you gifts," she said simply, her eyes twinkling.

Michael took her small hand in both of his. "No need, Sister Bird. You need not bring a gift. Just come. You are invited to the party."

Marissa felt a wave of sickness wash over her. Julie grasped his arm and smiled at Sister Bird. "You are welcome," Julie said. But her eyes gave away some fierce passion of possession. No one should talk to Michael. He was hers.

Only for a moment Marissa stood with them, her body and mind uncertain, her heart still pounding. She looked for someone to recognize what she was feeling. In this moment she tried to subdue her surprise, her leaping heart. Perhaps it would help if she recalled Blair. She tried to envision him, the sun-bleached strands of his choppy hair. She had tried to contact him. She had not seen him, and now it seemed he was in a different world. This crowd moving in line and shaking her hand, and laughing with Michael and Joey—this crowd of people around her that she knew and loved—this was the substance of her world as it had always been. And Blair was not there.

Fifteen

For the next few nights, Marissa stayed awake, unable to sleep because the last words of Carter and Morgan kept banging against the perimeter of her memory. She saw her brothers over and over again, standing on the threshold against the October light, the screen door creaking back and forth on its hinges. Both of them were in their overalls, stepping out into the brazen colors of leaves, ready to take the load of cantaloupes to town. "Do you want us to stop at the recorder's office and ask if they got them papers?" These were Carter's last words to her. For days, in her dreams, she could see Morgan tossing his hat on his head and waving goodbye, and Carter's narrow eyes in his sunburned face.

Michael hitched rides from the camp to come down that week before the funeral. He left the Chevrolet with Marissa because he wanted her to practice her driving, and to drive it to St. George to solve the property problems.

"We ought to get that done, Marissa," he said to her. "Can you get them to move a little faster? I don't understand what's taking so long. Do you know?"

In those moments she wanted to tell him everything. But for some reason it stuck in her throat. And when the subject came up again when he was down that week, Julie was there, hanging on his arm.

"I've tried to hurry them," Marissa answered him. "I missed this week because . . ."

"I know, Marissa."

"They keep wanting me to come back," she said, biting her lip to stop herself from blurting out, "Michael, it is possible I will be married before you. I cannot tell you what is truly going on. You would not believe me until it happens." But did *she* believe what was happening now? She was not absolutely sure. "I'm certain they are doing all they can do," she said. "I was supposed to go the day—the day after this happened."

"I know that." Michael dug his hands into his pockets. "Promise me that while I'm at work this week, you will drive the Chevrolet to St. George and try to get those papers for us? There's a possibility . . ."

What possibility?

"There's a possibility I can get a loan against our farm to finish school. We have to have those papers."

"All right, Michael. I promise."

Michael, Michael, Michael. I want you to go to school. I want everything you want. A degree in music so you can teach school. A wedding for you at Christmastime, if that's what you want. A family of wonderful children. Happiness. Did you know, Michael, that I am supposed to be married in two weeks on November 3, to the county recorder?

The words screamed at her. She heard them, she felt them, she swallowed them like some terrible medicine that clutched at her throat, burning on the way down. She felt paralyzed.

There was nothing she could do but follow Michael's plea. When Monday came she saw Wade walking in the yard, carrying tools to the barn. She put on her slippers and walked out onto the gravel.

"Is the Chevrolet safe to drive yet?" she asked him.

Wade was always a puzzle. He wore his dark hair plastered in a little V on his forehead. His curls seemed heavy on his neck beneath the flannel shirt. He seldom smiled. With a morose stare, he stopped to gaze at her. "Well, it ain't no new vehicle. You know that."

"I know that, Wade. I just want your opinion."

"You can get there." He cut his words short, seeming irritated and inconvenienced.

"The truck wasn't new, either," she said, just to think things through. "And we got there. You kept it in pretty good shape."

"Yes, ma'am," he murmured. "What do you think I been here so often for?"

He had other customers in Springdale, and he had still been there to see Maxine Riddle. But Marissa always had some subtle feelings about his hanging around the Rosefield place so much of the time. Joey felt it too.

"He's always someplace around here," her little brother said once. "I go down to the south boundary, and he busts up out of the grass like a mob of turkeys."

"He parks his car on the road to Springdale, so maybe he is just always walking through here to his car," Marissa speculated.

"Maybe he's just always over to Maxine Riddle's place," Joey said. "And I know why."

Everyone knew about Maxine, but no one wanted to say anything about it. Sister Riddle was sick over what had happened, and Brother Riddle wanted Maxine to get married and rescue some respectability for their family. Someone said Wade was from New York and lived with his sister in St. George. People from New York did not get married, but they dilly-dallied around, sleeping with different people, waiting to see if they were in love enough to make a commitment. If anyone asked Wade where he was from, he would not say much about it. He never talked about where he was living, so no one knew for sure. All they did know was that occasionally he drove the streets of Springdale with Maxine, and the two of them, like shadows, could sometimes be seen dragging a blanket behind a barn.

"I wish we could sell this place to the government, get a big fat check, and buy a new car so we wouldn't have to hire Wade," Joey said. "Sometimes he gives me the creeps."

Marissa was surprised to hear these words. "You want to sell the farm? But Father said . . ."

"I know what Father said. I am tired of being poor."

At night, Marissa thought about Joey's words. She had a dream that Michael and Julie were running to catch the train to go to school in Indiana, and Joey ran after them on the road, crying, "If you leave us, we'll sell the farm! We'll sell the farm!" In the dream, Marissa was running after them to Springdale, her skirts flapping in the breeze. She was crying out to them, "Please stop. Stop!" But if they heard her they did not stop to reply. The canyon walls bent over them like huge, monolithic beasts. She ran and ran, but could not catch up with Michael and Julie. When the sky began to swirl with dark clouds, Marissa saw her father's face come down like a light in the mist. His eyes were burning with a rose-colored fire. She woke, wondering what she had seen.

It was Wednesday before Marissa could talk herself into driving the Chevrolet to St. George. She was awake at four o'clock when the rooster began to crow. She heard Joey moving around in the boys' room, washing his face in the washroom, and opening and shutting the screen door as he went out to milk the cow. Joey was close to the same age the Prophet Joseph Smith was when he received his calling to discipline himself for a great work. At this tender age, Joey was now responsible for most of the work on the farm.

The farm. Marissa lay in bed to think for a while. She knew she must get up and drive to the city. But the sorrow that had dogged them all for so many weeks still seemed to lie over her like a pall, threatening to suffocate her.

When there was enough light through the window that she could see the Watchman, she reached for the books she kept on the bedside table, and randomly turned the pages. "All these things shall give thee experience, and shall be for thy good," God had told the Prophet Joseph Smith. *All these things,* Marissa said silently. There would someday be solace, light, peace. But she had to live for it, work for it, and have faith that it would happen.

She prayed silently that the Chevrolet would start, and after a little coaxing it did. Morgan and Carter had put enough gas in the tank to force the gauge to the top. As she backed noisily out of the barn and wheeled the old car around in the yard, she looked up to the red rocks under the October sky. Cumulus clouds bloomed like huge bales of raw cotton lying along the tops of the hills. They moved just enough across the brilliant blue of the sky to breathe life over the three Patriarch pinnacles, standing mute and heedful.

Trying to avoid the worst ruts as she steered, Marissa moved over to make way for a huge truck that was bringing another machine to the scene of the road Michael was building. Silently she said to herself, "Go, Michael. You are a road builder. Your perfect life will be exemplary in every way, and I wish I could be there to see it unfold into the eternities—into forever." Julie would be there. That was how it would be. But Marissa vowed she would always stay as close as she could.

At Springdale, the Chevrolet began to lurch, and she stopped at Madsen's gas pump to ask if Julius would just listen to it for a moment. He opened the hood and checked the wires. He told her he thought everything was good.

"But you never can tell, you know." As he shut the hood and fastened it down, he turned to her. "I don't know if you heard about this, but the Giffords that was inspecting the scene of your brothers' accident . . ." He hesitated. "They believe there was some fire powder in there."

Fire powder?

"In . . . in the truck?" Marissa wasn't sure she'd heard correctly. No one had ever said anything to cast any additional shadows over the tragedy that might bode for something even worse. No one had said, "There might have been something strange about this accident that you will someday discover, Marissa Rosefield. And when you do discover it, the entire world will change for you forever."

"Tom Gifford thought he smelled dynamite."

Dynamite? Marissa froze. Tom Gifford would know. He had used dynamite to blast out a hole in the hills of Rockville where the Stout brothers had moved their blind granny. She had lived in a dirt cave carved into a bank in the Oak Creek area, and when the National Parks Association purchased the land, the family used Tom's skill to blast out a hole in another bank so she would feel at home in the place where they had to move. In Oak Creek she used a rope to find her way to the outhouse, so they designed the same rope from cave to outhouse, and an extended one to the Stout home where the grandchildren looked for her to creep along the edge of the river when she came to visit. Tom had overseen several explosions along the roads that were built in 1917. Often whole rock cairns had to be blown to pieces so that the park busses and construction equipment could get through.

"I didn't know if you was acquainted with that discovery," Julius Madsen said quietly.

Marissa woke as though from a dream. "Uh . . ." she began. "No. No one told any of us there might have been some tampering with the truck."

"Your brothers ever use dynamite?" Julius asked.

Marissa felt stunned. But she tried to think back. "No . . . not that I can recall, but yes, maybe long ago." The memory flew above her thoughts and then lit on her mind like a live spark. Carter had used Gifford's dynamite to move one of the massive red stones in the orchard. He had seen the rock face on the Crawford property fall off the edge of the mountain of its own accord, and Gifford had offered to help them blow the huge piece into smithereens. It left the profile of a man that looked exactly like old Mr. Crawford. These incidents had taken place many years ago. But Marissa had never heard whether or not anyone had disposed of the dynamite. It was possible, she thought, that the boys had decided to sell their supply, or take it to some place where it could be safely destroyed. "I know they had some dynamite several years ago to move a piece of rock that intruded on the peach orchard. Maybe they decided to get that leftover powder out of the barn."

Julius looked vaguely unsettled, as though he knew more but could never disclose it. "Yes. Well, it's over now. There's no use to make an issue of something that will not bring your brothers back to you." When he closed the hood, he plunged his hands into the pockets of his overalls and said, "You know how sorry all of us are that this has happened."

"Yes," Marissa said. "Everyone's been kind. Thank you so much."

She felt the man's concern, but his circumspection did not match her panic. She was struck dumb. When she got back into the Chevrolet, she waited for a moment before she turned the key in the switch. *Dynamite?* Perhaps by some stretch of the imagination, some of that dynamite that had spilled in the barn may have made its way into the old truck. And possibly the Chevrolet?

Why hadn't someone said something about this suspicion to Michael? Or perhaps they had, and he hadn't wanted to bring up the subject to her or to Joey, because it might mean the accident, the deaths, might have been prevented. And Michael was planning to get married and move as far away from here as he could. He would bury himself in the musical classics, play in the orchestra, and never touch the complexities of this tragic event again. And Marissa could not blame him for that. But if by some subtlety there would someday be discovered that some responsibility for the explosion lay with someone who might be blamed for a murderous act . . . the consequences flared up in her imagination with terrible implications. And fear. She remembered she was supposed to have been in that truck the day of the accident. But she shook her head and put it out of her mind. What was she thinking? She was dreaming up all kinds of causes and effects with preposterous ramifications. She would pray, she would have faith. And she would get to St. George in one piece, she was sure.

When she stopped the motor in the county court's parking lot, she breathed a sigh of relief. But then, in the shadows in back of the courthouse, with the air thick and still, the quiet became almost oppressive. She waited inside the Chevy, still leaning forward, when behind her she watched another car drive up the hill and into the back parking lot. She stayed quiet while the driver got out. It was a woman. It looked like Bruzy.

It *was* Bruzy.

The bleached-blond secretary opened the door of the car and slid out. She shut the driver's door and opened the back. With some difficulty she lifted a large box into her arms. It was wrapped loosely in an old red plaid tablecloth, and tied around one side only with a rope that looked like it was about to come loose. She had trouble shutting the back door of the car, but she backed up to it and hit it with her hip.

Marissa did not want to run into Bruzy, so she waited. She might have held the door for the woman—it looked like Bruzy was struggling under the load. Though Marissa felt she could have helped, she stayed put. She watched while Bruzy kicked one knee up under the box so she could have a hand to open the door of the court house, backed into the door to keep it open, and slid into the back hallway.

Marissa did not understand the darkness that settled over her. She waited a few more minutes before gathering herself together, pulling at her gloves and clutching her bag. The walk to the courthouse seemed miles long, every footstep uncertain.

Once she was inside the back door, she walked a little faster. It would not do for her to appear faint-hearted when she greeted Mrs. Montgomery. Marissa could see the edge of the receptionist's desk as she walked into the hall.

"Did you get some of it copied, Bruzy?" It was Mrs. Montgomery's voice.

"I did. I'll probably have to take it home again to finish it up, though. Blair didn't want me to leave it where anybody else could get to it." There was a pause while Bruzy must have hoisted the box into a better position, although Marissa could not see. "My brother is the nosy type—ha," Bruzy said, breathing heavily under the weight.

Marissa wasn't sure why, but she stopped before making herself known. She knew she was eavesdropping, but she couldn't help herself. She heard Bruzy shuffle behind the receptionist's desk. She heard her slam the bundle on the desk behind the archway.

"Got more?" It was Blair's voice from the recorder's room.

"Yes," Bruzy said. "Did you read what I brought yesterday?"

If he answered her, it was with such quiet words that Marissa did not hear. She concentrated so intently on what was happening in the recorder's rooms, she did not notice Mrs. Montgomery stepping away from her desk, walking to a cupboard in the hallway, and rifling through some papers. When she finally picked them up to carry to her desk, she looked up briefly.

"Oh! Miss Rosefield!" she said. "I didn't know you were here! Did you make an appointment?"

"No," Marissa said.

Mrs. Montgomery put the papers in her left hand and beckoned with her right. "Come on in. We haven't seen you for a while. I'm sure Mr. Harper will be happy to see you. They're in his office. I'll ring him. Come, wait here for a few minutes."

It seemed to be the longest wait of Marissa's life. She picked up the *National Geographic Magazine,* but it was full of earthquake, devastation, and the faces of impoverished children caught in misery under patches of swarming insects and flies. She put it down and pulled at the fringes of her gloves.

Mrs. Montgomery hung up the phone. "He'll be available in a moment." She looked up. "I was so sorry to read in the paper about the accident. And your brothers—both of them. I'm so sorry. Oh my, it is a terrible thing that happened."

Marissa tried to smile. "Thank you." *Yes, it is.*

The door through the hallway opened. Marissa was in a chair that sat opposite the hall to the suite. She could see Bruzy leave Blair's office to walk into her own. She looked like a wild woman, her hair frowzy, her face flushed, her eyes glazed. When she disappeared behind the door to the archives, Blair's door finally opened.

"Marissa," he said.

That was all.

She took each step separately as though if she did not concentrate, she would fall.

He said nothing else until she entered his office and closed the door. The light streaming through the colored glass revealed a bough of dry leaves bobbing under the weight of a small bird. The light in the office warmed Marissa instantly, as though the fire they had shared was still burning there. But at the same time, she could also feel something cold.

No words came until she and Blair faced one another across the desk.

"Where were you?" he finally asked.

There was a moment of silence before she could gather her thoughts. "Didn't Bruzy tell you?"

"Tell me what?" He was irritated. He looked through the strand of bleached and straw-colored hair that sometimes fell across his eyes. He did not move but sat waiting, his elbow on the arm of the chair.

"I called Bruzy. Didn't you read about the accident in Springdale?"

"What accident?"

She was shocked. He had heard nothing?

"I expected you to come sometime last week," he said between his teeth. "I waited for you. November 3rd is a week and a half away. I thought you had changed your mind. I'm not sure this is . . ."

Marissa's mind began to spin in a hundred directions. "So you didn't know my brothers were killed?"

"What?" Blair leaned forward in his chair, put his elbows on his desk, and focused on her face with wide-eyed alarm. "What happened?"

"You didn't see? It was in the newspaper. I hoped you would come to the funeral."

"Marissa, no!"

For a moment she felt blinded by light, by the intensity of the air.

"Both of your brothers were killed? What happened?"

"The truck. It exploded on the road to Virgin." She hesitated, lowering her eyes, but he did not say anything to fill the quiet.

When she raised her gaze, she saw he had leaned back in the chair again and held his hand over his eyes. "Marissa." Her name seemed lost in his mouth. "I'm sorry."

She remained quiet, trying to read everything—his face almost hidden behind his hair, the light in the transom, the withered boughs. The bird had flown away.

"I don't read the St. George papers," he finally murmured. "I wish I had known. No, Bruzy didn't tell me." He paused, then shook the hair out of his eyes and put both hands on the edge of the desk. "Marissa, I'm so sorry." He stood and walked around the desk to her. "Will you forgive me?" He took her hand, the arm of her chair. "I would have been there." He lifted her hand and enclosed it with both of his. Marissa . . ." He pulled her to her feet. Tears crowded her eyes and spilled onto her cheeks. She wiped them away with her right hand.

"Marissa, Marissa, Marissa Rosefield, come here." He took her in his arms. The light from the panes of glass fell across the desk and flickered like flames of stoked coals. She felt some barrier somewhere. He held her, but a strange shade of spirit prevented her from responding. "We are together just in time," he whispered. "Marissa. You are still with me?" He pulled back and brushed the hair from her eyes. "You haven't told anyone, have you?"

She saw the question in his face, his eyes narrow. "No," she said.

“Good. We’ll keep it quiet for a while.”

When he kissed her, there was tenderness in it, but no fire. She felt uneasy, yet when he pulled her closer, she stayed in his arms.

Sixteen

On the drive home, Marissa didn't think about the car, whether or not it would make it through Hurricane, La Verkin, Toquerville, Rockville, Springdale—all the little towns between St. George and the farm. The hills loomed like blue and mottled dunes rising in the distance along the south side of the river. She could see for a hundred miles under the cobalt sky.

The river at the bend shimmered with the reflection of the afternoon sun—so iridescent, the glare from the water seemed to blister her eyes. She pulled down the visor from above the windshield, but the reflection from the water below still struck her, making it terribly difficult to see. When trucks or cars came at her on the other side of the road, Marissa slowed and hugged the edge. But the bumps through the weeds rattled the Chevy with such force that she crawled back onto the gravel.

She could not put away her uneasy feelings—a gnawing unrest that would not subside—even while she entered the canyon and again felt safe inside the towering red walls that kept the vexatious world away. Was she willing to leave all of this? Perhaps more disturbing, would Blair ever share it with her? It belonged to another life—the life she had known all these years with the Rosefield family. More than anything, Marissa feared losing the warmth, the memories: playing duets with Michael, scraping honey out of the hive and mixing it with peanut butter, smelling the bread baking in the oven, throwing leftover carrots to the chickens, gathering warm eggs in the cold mornings, pruning the grapes in a January frost.

She remembered when she was ten, her mother made herself a dress for the Gold and Green Ball out of an old purple curtain. Ellen put her hair high up on her head, and Papa said to Marissa, "Your mother is the most beautiful woman in the world." Then they received the letter from Mother's cousin Dan Groberg, explaining that his son Chase had been killed in the world war and had written in his will that he wanted to leave his bassoon to Michael. Chase had come through from California for a visit and heard Michael play the saxophone one night in a kids' band at church. "I won't be blowing horns no more," Chase wrote. "Michael is talented. Give my bassoon to him."

After the instrument came by rail and then wagon to the post office, Bertie Smith had called and said, "There's a big box here for Michael Rosefield." When Papa brought it to the house, the family surrounded it, peering into the blue-velvet-lined case. But they didn't touch the bassoon. Michael wasn't daunted, however. He managed to put the mouthpiece together and make noise. He practiced until the sound was sweet and direct—reminiscent of a piper in the hills of a faraway country, a sound that pierced the blue sky and shivered in the sage-covered peaks under the blazing sun.

The following Christmas, Marissa asked for a cello. Papa hid it in the barn until Christmas morning, when the brothers brought it into the house, carrying it in a tarp they had used to harvest cantaloupes, gathering all four corners and lugging them to the bed of the truck.

All of life changes. Mama and Papa were gone. And now Morgan and Carter were gone. Marissa had run to them, laughing because as they cradled the tarp, they bounced it while they sang softly, "What child is this . . ."

Papa laughed too. That was long ago. Mama cut up the apples and loaded them into a crust sprinkled with cinnamon. The smell of the apples and cinnamon cooking inside the pie crust infused the atmosphere with the proper ambience for a squeaky cello, a sweet bassoon, and the Christmas spirit.

When Marissa drove into the yard, Joey waved to her. He was chopping wood. His face was red.

Joey. Joey. Joey. Her thoughts were of Blair's words. He had said, "We'll spend the first week on a honeymoon. Then when Michael leaves for school, we'll move to the farm and take care of Joey."

Not that Joey needed much care. He was almost sixteen years old. The deaths had changed him—had changed all of them. And because Michael was working and leaving, Joey was in charge of the farm now. It was an immediate transformation. One day he was a child, and the next day he was an adult, taking full responsibility for everything. For a moment, Marissa watched him concentrate on where he pounded the ax to chop the kindling. She was so grateful Blair would stay on the farm. At least he said he would come to live at the Rosefield house when he was able to feel totally organized. For a while, he hoped, she would not mind staying in the small basement he now rented from the manager of the cotton mill.

The week ahead of her loomed like a dream she could not catch. The old Indians used to weave "dream catchers." They bent a flexible reed into a small or large circle, bound the circle with a strip of leather, and wove small strands of hemp or string across the circle, creating a net through which a dream could be caught. The images of Christmas, the harvest, of Mother and Papa smiling while she began playing—all of it passed through Marissa's thoughts, then slipped through the net of her memory, like dreams through the red hills she was leaving now.

The time passed so slowly, she could not piece together what she was doing in the kitchen with the thoughts of Blair, and what was to happen on November 3rd with no one else in the area—no one in Springdale, no one in Rockville or Grafton—knowing what was happening. Not even Joey. And Michael was always in the camp now, working hard for his future. If she had tried to open her mouth to anyone, some lock in Marissa's lips would not let her speak.

She remodeled her mother's purple dress. At least she would wear something memorable. She would cut the salvia away from the stems and make a bouquet, though it would not last. She knew she could explain to Joey that she must once more go into St. George to the courthouse and take the Chevy through Springdale, Rockville, Virgin, La Verkin, Toquerville, Hurricane—the distance seemed to mesmerize her. She had packed her things. And she wrote a note to Joey: "Don't wait for me. They told me I must stay in town a few nights for some legal procedure to produce title to the land. I will get in touch with you through Bertie's post-office phone very soon."

She abandoned the hills, the broad land, Joey. Everything moved past her in slow motion. She concentrated on the Chevrolet. Wade said he had put a new belt on the brakes on Saturday.

The silence in town was oppressive. Nothing moved. There was no traffic at 10:00 AM. Occasionally a withered leaf fell from a tree. It seemed Marissa had made her way through the archway to Blair a hundred times. Mrs. Montgomery wasn't there. Bruzy and Tessie were not there. Only Mr. Scott worked in the back corner. Marissa had a terrible feeling Blair was not there. So when he opened his door, she heard herself breathe a sigh of relief.

He was smiling. He was warm. He reached for her hand. He led her into the office while he finished what he was doing. Then he looked up at her and asked, "Are you ready?"

He led her out into the hall and toward the back of the building to the courtroom. Two older men Marissa had never seen before stood at the far end, smiling as they greeted her and Blair. The court secretary sat at a small desk.

"So this is the lovely lady," one of the older men said.

It was over in an instant. The papers were signed. The words were said. "You may kiss as man and wife."

Blair leaned over Marissa and gathered her into his arms. When he brought her close and kissed her, her head swam with light. He took a small box out of his pocket and put a ring on her finger. "My little farm girl," he whispered through her curls.

In the car again, he told her where they were going. "I've made arrangements for our honeymoon night in a lodge on St. George Boulevard."

She laughed. "You are full of surprises."

"I am," he said.

The lodge was the nicest of the two motels in St. George, shaped in a U with a pool in the front yard.

"Did you bring your swimming suit?" Blair wondered.

"No." She hadn't thought of it.

"Well, no matter." He smiled at her. "We'll be busy doing other things." He winked.

The white tile in the foyer dazzled her eyes. Blair was brisk with the clerk, almost to the point of embarrassing Marissa.

"Did you do what I asked—about the flowers?" he asked.

"The flowers?" the clerk said. "Did we get that message? Perhaps someone else took that message . . ."

"Some service," Blair murmured.

Marissa tried to overlook the tone of his voice. He was undoubtedly as nervous as she was.

Their room was clean. Dark drapes striped with alternating patterns of red satin and autumn leaves hung at the windows.

One painting hung above the bed on the wall, a pink and beige Mexican hacienda glowing in the twilight. Everything else in the room matched the painting: the bed cover, the deep maroon in the rug, the faded pink towels in the bathroom. Marissa had never been in such a place.

"Do you like it?" Blair asked.

"It's pretty." She smiled.

"I had flowers ordered, but evidently they didn't come."

When he turned to her, she was surprised. She had barely placed her suit bag on the bed when he began to pull away her coat. "At last," he said. "I've been waiting for this for a long time."

What? What was he doing?

"Come here," he said.

She didn't know what else she could do but obey him. He leaned over and kissed her. "Do you know what this kind of kissin' means?" He smiled.

"We're man and wife."

"You got it," he said like a coach praising his first baseman for a good catch.

For a few moments, Marissa believed him. She responded to his embrace, to the disrobing, when he opened the sheets and led her to the bed. She lived on a farm. She knew what was going to happen. She was not ignorant of these things. But she was taken back by Blair's speed. He kissed her. She felt warm in his arms.

"After this I'll order from the Chinese buffet," he whispered, pushing back her hair.

But the dinner never came.

When she looked back on these moments she blamed herself. She was married. She should have given herself fully. But the pain hit her so hard, her entire body lurched backward.

"Damn!" He pulled back. "Impossible." He swore.

Marissa cowered. It looked like he would hit her. The room filled with a black cloud.

"I should have guessed." He rose and hunted for his clothes. "The drugstore is probably open." She lay still on the bed, not moving. "Lotion, or oil," he mumbled.

He did not come back until 4:00 AM.

She was sleeping. When she heard the key in the lock and the door opened, she was startled awake. But she didn't move. She watched the dark figure enter the room. Her heart pumped with a booming sound that seemed to bounce off the ceiling.

"Marissa, I'm sorry. I was so ready. You got me excited, baby," he crooned. When he lay beside her, he began touching her again. "We'll try again," he said, lying beside her in the faded glow from the pole lights around the pool. "I'm sorry. I brought something that will help."

It worked. But the shock of all that had happened had already done its damage to her heart. The light had begun to weaken outside the windows. When Blair finally fell asleep beside her, she lay in pain, terrified, too paralyzed even to cry. She stared at the Motel sign outside the window. Her mind jogged from the orchard to the patch of cabbages. Michael had always said they looked like flowers. "You have to peel away all of that outside stuff to get to the heart of it." He would stand out in the field with the others and make a game of the harvest, tossing the big, cream-colored cabbages, which looked like huge roses, to Carter. In turn, Carter often rolled them into the back of the truck like bowling balls.

The truck. It was gone. Carter was gone. Morgan was gone. Marissa's mother and father were gone. The night closed in on her like a huge sponge.

Seventeen

The woman came down out of the Grand Canyon without her new husband. That was what Marissa remembered best about old Bertie Smith's story that night long ago when they camped out at the Sinewava. It was so dark, even the moon was having a difficult time emerging from behind black clouds. All of the ward members had brought sleeping bags and lined them up in rows for the campout. They sang "Springtime in the Rockies" and "Yankee Doodle Went to Town." Jeb Robinson, Julie's brother, played the ukulele. That was before he went to the war in France and lost his leg. They gathered so close around the fire that the light on their faces shone like golden globes, or golden apples hanging from a ring of trees.

The woman came down from the campground on the top of the South Rim of Zion with a bruise on her cheek. As Michael reminded Marissa of the story later, he said the woman's name was Bessie.

When the townspeople asked her where her husband was, Bessie had looked at them with glazed eyes. Her coat was torn at the collar, and the edges were singed with charcoal. "I don't know," she said.

A week later, Bertie said he and Angus Woodsboro decided they ought to go to the South Rim and look for him. All they could find was a black frying pan in a pit of charred wood that looked like it had been doused by a rainstorm. A few yards beyond that, they found a tent, pulled up on three of its stakes, leaning over like a tired piece of laundry that came undone from its line. Inside the tent, they found the body of the bridegroom. His head had been flattened, and the dried blood swarmed with maggots.

"She smashed his head with the frying pan," Bertie whispered. "But we knew him, so Angus and I didn't say anything."

Cold gripped Marissa's neck.

The two days she and Blair spent in the motel began to feel better. The light coming in between the striped draperies rose and sank like moving beacons on a cargo ship. Blair vacillated between moods of sweet gallantry and angry outbursts. He railed at the waiter in the Summit Steak House because the napkin got dipped in the gravy. "I don't tip them when they are so clumsy," he whispered to Marissa. "Honestly, I wanted to make this perfect, and some of it's turned out to be an absolute sham."

During their steak dinner, Blair leaned over to her and said, "My wedding present is a surprise for you."

She paused in the middle of a bite of baked potato.

He smiled. The light from the window seemed to drop in that moment into a purple shadow.

"A surprise?" she said.

"You didn't think I'd let our wedding go without a present, did you?"

Marissa had failed to outguess him, so she laughed. "What is the surprise?"

"I'm not telling. On our way to my place, I'll stop at the office and show you."

The candles on the table flickered. She saw his eyes brighten and thought, *I believe I am in love with him, and it will just have to work itself out.*

In the car, he reached over and took her hand. It was the first moment Marissa felt the same fire she had felt under the light from the transom in his office. When they reached the courthouse, Blair followed her past the front desk and through the archway. "You will be amazed. I've saved it all this time for you," he said.

The key seemed clumsy in the lock of his office, the door heavy.

"Now, wait for me," he said in a sly voice.

Marissa sat in the same chair she had always used when she had come to visit with him. Blair left her to go into the other office for a moment. There was no light in the transom. There was no color from the stained glass on the desktop. There was no Mrs. Montgomery, Bruzy, Tessie, or Mr. Scott. The courthouse was silent with the mute ringing of the hundreds of voices that had filled it for half a century.

When he came back to her, Blair was carrying a charred metal box. The patina had been scarred with what looked like years of abrasion and weather. He laid the box on the desk, sat across from her, put his elbows on the edge, and rested his chin on his hands. "Bet you don't know what this is."

Marissa swallowed. No, she didn't know.

"We found your box," he said.

My box? For a moment she did not understand what he meant, so she sat still, waiting for him to explain. But even before he opened his mouth, she realized. The truth came for her at the speed of a freight train. She stayed quiet, her mind turning over and over with questions.

"My box?"

"You remember." Blair leaned forward in his chair. "Your father buried the box at the Watchman."

She felt the top of her head tighten. "Blair! You . . . you . . ."

"Right." He grinned. "We found it."

The next question was really unnecessary, and she felt stupid after she asked it. "Where?"

"At the Watchman." Blair smiled heartily with a trace of teasing.

"H–h–how?" she stammered.

"That's for me to know, and for you to find out," he taunted.

The moment was electric. "I . . . I can't believe it!" she said. "Blair! That's amazing!" She remembered Bruzy carrying something heavy into the courthouse. Now the woman's conversation with Mrs. Montgomery made sense.

Blair sat back in his chair. "Yes, it is amazing. It was brought to us by someone who could not open it, and they wondered if it was important. And voilà!" He paused. "It was!" It seemed like an eternity before he continued. "And we have looked at all the papers and found some interesting things."

Marissa's skin crawled. He had kept this from her for a long time. Why? "Oh, Blair! I wish you had told me about this the minute—"

He interrupted her. "No. It's your wedding gift. There are some special things I want you to understand." He paused, probably for effect. "Are you ready to hear them?"

"Yes. Yes, of course!" She sat forward. "So you can verify the Rosefields' ownership of the farm?"

Blair waited a moment, clearly enjoying the effect of his surprise. Everything seemed to be moving—the light, the clouds through the transom, the moon.

"Your ownership," he said.

For a moment it was quiet.

"Do you understand?" He leaned forward again.

"No. *My* ownership?"

"Yes, *your* ownership," Blair said, massaging the words with his tongue. "You are now the owner of the Rosefield property.

Well, as soon as Joey reaches the age of eighteen, he will share in the ownership."

She didn't understand. *Michael. What about Michael?* "But Michael . . ."

"That is one of the surprises I have for you," Blair replied. "It's about Michael."

What about him? Marissa's fingers grew sore from clutching her hands so tightly in her lap.

Blair leaned over the box and pried the lid loose with a fingernail file. The box croaked at the hinges. It sounded like a scream. Dust from the old paint rose into the lamplight.

He plunged into the papers. "Michael is not a Rosefield," Blair said. He withdrew a small journal covered with black cloth and tied with a faded yellow ribbon. The binding was broken, the backs of the sewn folios stained with age. He untied the ribbon and opened the book carefully at a place marked with a modern picture postcard from someone he must have known in New York City. "I want you to read this," he said quietly. "It belonged to your mother, Ellen."

The words were scrawled with lead so thick, they were barely readable. *I found Michael in the flood, but I knew he wasn't mine. My Michael was never found. I have always loved the little boy I raised. I have kept the secret all these years.*

Marissa's heart lurched. She caught herself at the edge of the desk. She read the words again. They were in her mother's handwriting. *Incredible.*

Blair took some other documents from the box. "This is the will. Michael isn't on it."

Marissa couldn't believe it. When Blair handed it to her, she missed taking it the first time because her hand was trembling.

Why? Did Papa Bradley know? Who was Michael, then? Bird's little boy who was lost in the river? Jim Owen's son?

Jim, the great hunter who had slain so many cougars, bears, and bobcats for the safety of the Grand Canyon? Tessie's sister?

Her heart leaped in her throat. "I . . . I wondered why you took so long . . ." she managed to murmur.

"You can do whatever you want with it now." Blair smiled. He sat back in his chair. "If you wanted to sell it, it is worth enough money to keep you for the rest of your life." He was still smiling when he rocked back in the chair and put his hands behind his head.

For a few moments, Marissa tried to assimilate what had just happened. Her world was spinning, clanging, like a string of freight cars through a noisy tunnel, the news deafening. It was hard to breathe. She gasped when her thoughts crashed into daylight, as though the sun suddenly exploded in her brain.

Michael was not her blood brother! That was what hit her when she sat staring at her husband across his desk in the office of the Washington County Courthouse. Michael had always been different from the Rosefields. He was an outsider. She couldn't grasp it. All these years! He had always been darker, as though he belonged to another world. He had talent none of the others had. He was kinder, gentler. He always spoke with a subdued voice, never yelling. Papa, Carter, and Morgan had yelled. The instrument Michael held gently in his long fingers always responded to his breath with the purest, most resonant sound. And Marissa had loved him.

The revelation hit her with a stunning force. She reeled as she watched Blair thumb through the pages of a book he was reading to her.

"It was written on bad paper," he said. "The paper didn't hold up in the ground. It almost fell apart. There were holes in it. It has a few unreadable spots. But it will hold up in court."

She read the dusty pages—the list of names without a mention of Michael's. She glanced at the faded sprawl of Ellen's handwriting again. *Michael, Michael, Michael,* Marissa thought. *All these years I loved you. And not just like a brother.*

Blair was still thumbing through documents. "Since Michael's going to Indiana, we can sell the property to the government to enhance Zion National Park. They wanted it to build a great information center and museum."

Marissa sat frozen, thoughts racing through her head. When she did not answer him, Blair looked up from the desk. "Are you all right, Marissa?"

She swallowed.

"Just shocked?" He smiled one of his gentle smiles. "I've known about this for some time. I just didn't want to upset you." He paused. "Does it upset you, Marissa? I thought you would be glad . . ."

She wasn't sure. Everything in her life seemed to be moving so fast.

"You are okay with this, aren't you?"

She gazed at him. "I . . . I guess so." What else could she have said? The moment felt as heavy as granite.

"You and Joey won't want to farm the place all by yourselves." Blair leaned over the desk and reached for her hand. After a moment, to avoid trouble, she gave it to him. "It's time to let the farm go, Marissa. I'm sorry." He smiled. "You and I will have enough money to buy a house in town, free and clear. I have a good job. I promise you a great future, Marissa."

"There was something," she said. "Michael was . . ." She stopped, her mouth dry.

"Yes, what about Michael?"

No, she thought. *Nothing. You would never understand. Do even I understand?*

“Yes? What about Michael?” Blair repeated, then paused. “If you wish, we can help him . . .”

“He was going to try to take out a loan on the farm.” Marissa’s tongue seemed swollen. “He needed help to go to school in Indiana.”

“Sure.” Blair let go of her hand. He leaned back in his chair as though he had already assumed the comfort of wealth. “Now he can go to school without debt hanging over his head. You can tell him we’ll help.” He smiled. “We’ll help him, Marissa.”

She was very much aware it was now “we.” She found her tongue and murmured, “Michael and Julie would appreciate it.” A rock was sitting in her stomach. She saw Blair through a haze. “May . . . may I tell him, by myself,” she said softly, “when he comes down from the camp on Saturday?”

“Sure, sure.” Blair nodded. He offered her a broad smile and again reached for her hand.

Eighteen

A tic at the window woke Marissa early on Saturday morning. She wondered if a bird had flown into the glass. Awake now, she reoriented herself. They had moved into Blair's apartment, a musty basement that smelled like cigarette smoke. Small windows with ill-fitting brown shades let in some light from the street. The kitchen was cluttered. "Didn't have time to clean it up," Blair said. Marissa had poured some Ivory soap on a rag and scrubbed the dishes.

Today was the day she had been given permission to go home to talk to Michael. The prospect plagued her. A demon was present like some vast, undetermined substance pressing against her until she could hardly breathe.

Blair's place was so small she could sit up and reach the shade above the bed and make a slit of daylight broad enough to see. The dawn was deep purple, the sun still far away. She slipped from the covers into the narrow space between the bed and the wall—quietly, so she would not wake Blair. She found her slippers and padded to the bathroom. Because it was adjacent to the bedroom, she waited until she shut the door to turn on the light. She did not know if she should dare to flush the toilet.

"Aghhh . . ." She heard Blair's cry as a protest of some dark nightmare.

When she stepped out of the bathroom, she left the light on and kept the door open a crack so she could see to hunt for her clothes. She reached for her sweater. In the bleak light, she saw her husband raise his head and take his watch from the side table.

"What? What the . . ." He swore in words she was not used to hearing—even from him. They struck her like a volley of stones.

"What?" He read the time. "It's 4:45 in the morning!" Then more sharply, "Marissa! Where the heck are you going?"

She quickly turned out the light in the bathroom. The room flooded with darkness except for a sliver of light from the street struggling through the crack of the window shade.

"It's Saturday morning!"

"I know it's Saturday morning. It's an ungodly hour!" He hit the bed. "Get back here right now . . ."

"I need to—"

"What? Why could you possibly be getting up at quarter to five? This is still our honeymoon! Come here!"

When he continued to strike the bed and speak unspeakable words, she stood torn, shaken by the cold, by the draft seeping through the corners of the walls.

"Remember, you said I could go to tell Michael—so that he knows everything. He'll be back from the camp this morning."

"You that anxious to get home?" Blair raised his head then. "I know. You want to get back—to what, I don't know. An empty house except for a kid who doesn't care anyway! I know, you're homesick. Well, you'll get back soon enough. Now come here!" He reached for her hand. His eyes lowered to her sweater. "Take it off, girl!"

She was still shaking. She couldn't believe it. The half hour that followed seemed like something out of a melodramatic silent film. She couldn't understand what had happened to her feelings. Her heart just wasn't in her lovemaking. She submitted to Blair because she did not want to rouse his anger. But she couldn't do much more than pretend that she cared.

The moments passed slowly. She was still in pain. "Blair . . ."

"Yeah, I know. You were hankerin' to get to your precious brothers." He rolled over, ready to go back to sleep. "Yeah, yeah. It showed. You were about as exciting as a wet noodle." He nuzzled down into his pillow. "Yeah. I told you, go ahead and take the car. The keys are in my pants. So get out! Go! Get it over with!"

Marissa practically limped out of the apartment to the parking lot. She was hurting. With tears welling up in her eyes, she fumbled for the keys. As she drove Blair's car out to the street, she was aware more than ever of the dark skies, the purple rim of clouds, the sweeping fields along the bench. The distant rim of blue hills visible in the morning light seemed to hypnotize her.

What had happened? What had she done to marry Blair in the offices of the county courthouse? Had she been so overwhelmed with the power of her own passion? And was that enough of a reason to marry the man who came along and seemed to want her? The pain swirled in her head. She felt so confused. She hoped that when she came back later, he would be the person she believed she knew. Never again did she want to encounter the man who woke with uncontrolled anger in the middle of the night. What had happened? She did not know, except for one fact. She knew her bed had been made. She was Mrs. Harper. She had signed an agreement, spoken a vow, entered into a contract. But on the drive through the half-lit boulevard, the vast sage-crusted open range, through the tiny towns of Hurricane and La Verkin, she felt the pull of her farm home as she had never felt it before—an overwhelming homesickness and a sudden regret. It surprised her when the tears continued to fill her eyes and spill down her cheeks.

At the mouth of the canyon—after Virgin, Rockville, Springdale—when the red vision of the Watchman loomed over her, Marissa lost control of her emotions and began to sob. She pulled over to the side of the road. She didn't want Michael to see her like this. Ahead of her, the Patriarchs stood like three circumspect judges, waiting, waiting, as they had waited for eons of time—ever since the molten rocks had heaved and boiled to the surface of the earth. Eons of time. She was a speck. A mite of history. The Patriarchs—the vast monoliths—were not aware she was torn with anguish. The stones of the earth were not aware that her mind was heavy, nagging at her—that she was entertaining the heartbreaking suspicion that it was possible she was married to the wrong person! Had she made a hasty decision? There was no longer any simple equation. *Michael, Michael. We were so careful. And all this time . . .*

She waited on the road for what seemed like forever. But nothing became clearer to her. As the huge trucks lumbered past, she grew uneasy. One of them stopped, and a dirty-faced man in the passenger seat leaned out the window. "Do you need help, ma'am?"

Yes, I need help, she thought. *But not the kind of help you could even imagine.*

She shook her head.

"Well, then, good luck, ma'am."

After the truck pulled away, a Model T Ford with blaring headlights stopped behind her. There was enough daylight now to see the burly man who opened the door on the driver's side and lumbered toward her. It wasn't the police, was it? No. She thought she recognized the car from somewhere. The man was wearing a blue cap with a bill on it, and his curly hair was a shaggy, dark mop that looked like it had just received a shock of electricity.

He probably thought she was in trouble. If she could, she would just drive away right now. But when she tried to start the car again, the motor would not turn over. For a moment she felt terrified.

"What's wrong, lady?"

She breathed a sigh of relief and wiped her face. It was Wade Keller.

"What in the heck is going on?" he asked. "You in trouble?"

She rolled down the window. "You used to have that little, broken-down car. I never saw you in this one."

"Oh, Marissa Rosefield!" he said as if surprised. He laid his hand on the window. "I been usin' my sister's car. She don't need it on Saturdays. I been doin' mechanical work at the camp."

"I'm glad it was just you."

"I heard you try to start it. Your engine sounds like it's out of gas."

"I . . ." she began.

But he leaned into the window and interrupted her. "Hey, this looks like a car I seen before. Looks like a gov'ment car . . ."

How does he know? Something like a dark shadow crept over her. She tried to start the engine again, but it sputtered. It was true, she was out of gas.

"I'll drive you back to Bertie Smith's gas station," Wade drawled. "I got a can."

"Oh, thank you. That would be good."

When she climbed out of the car, he seemed to loom over her like the mountains she saw ahead. He did not seem to back away from her, but hovered too close, and she felt suffocated.

She was glad it was just Wade. But what had happened in the last moment? Something was wrong. Dreadfully wrong. How had he guessed she was driving a government car? When she opened his passenger door, she again puzzled over what he was driving, but she couldn't say why it seemed so familiar. She climbed into the car and sat as far against the window as she could. She wanted to get the gas in the can, gas up Blair's automobile, and get away as soon as possible. But the silence begged her to fill it with something.

"This is your sister's car?"

Wade had one arm in the window of the driver's door, and the other hovering over the top of the wheel. He glanced at her. "Yeah," he said without elaboration.

"I heard once that you live with your sister in town?"

Wade looked straight ahead on the road. "Yeah. Few blocks from the courthouse. She works for the gov'ment."

"Oh," Marissa said. And suddenly she knew. She recognized the car. It was the same old Ford that Bruzy backed out of with the box quite a while ago—the critical box wrapped in the checkered cloth. Bruzy had backed up to the courthouse door, butted the door open, and taken the box through the hallway . . . to Blair.

Marissa watched Wade's eyes. He looked straight ahead. Did he know what he had just revealed? She wasn't sure, but she kept quiet. He seemed to feel uncomfortable and began to chatter.

"I work on the camp's gov'ment equipment on Saturdays." He glanced at a watch he had tied around his wrist with a strip of leather. "I'll still make it if we stop at Bertie Smith's and fill the can."

"Wade, I can't tell you how much I appreciate this."

"Oh, it's nothin'. I been workin' for Mr. Bradley since your mother died. I owe you somethin'."

What came over her like a black pall? Something . . . something was wrong. She tried to dismiss it as just her worry about talking to Michael. But questions began batting at her. She prayed Michael would be at the house. She prayed with all the prayer she had left in her heart, hoping to move heaven and earth. She had so much to tell him.

Bertie seemed surprised to see Wade in the store. "You just barely got gas here," he said.

"I know. I'm helpin' Marissa Rosefield fill up. Her car is up the road apiece. It run out of gas."

"Wade has been helping us since my mother died," Marissa told Bertie.

"Yes, I know," he said. He was jovial and helpful. But after Wade helped her fill the can and she paid for the gas, the storekeeper narrowed his eyes. It was a strange look, as though he suspected something not quite right. Did he think she and Wade had some other connection? Marissa felt an anxiety she did not understand.

"Thank you, Bertie," she said when the money had exchanged hands.

On the drive back to her car, there was a leaden silence.

"Thank you so much, Wade," she said again, as he put the lid on the gas can. "You've saved me this morning!"

"Think nothin' of it." He didn't smile. He just tipped his hat, got back into Bruzy's car, and drove away.

Nineteen

She heard it before she reached the orchard—a faint sound, a whisk on the air, almost as unidentifiable as the shuffle of dry leaves still hanging from their sharp vines. At first Marissa thought it was her imagination. She had been traumatized this morning by so much, it had pitched her into a state of unrest.

What was it? But she knew. The nearer she drew to the driveway, the clearer the sound. It was "Träumarei." It rose, it throbbed, the notes cascaded over one another until it fell, only once more to begin the same refrain, the melody as pure and as straight as the toll of a bell. It was an accompaniment to all that had happened this morning, an omen of huge proportions. It could have been relief, but it was a knell of foreboding. She was about to tell Michael everything! Magic touched the top of her head where the nerves danced under her hair.

Wait for me. Hold the spell. The music echoed in the red stones like some ancient native ceremony. Spirits surrounded the rocks as the waft of a mist, or the overwhelming odor of violets. It came through the canyon like a symphony—or the voice of angels.

As the car slowed on the driveway, Marissa rolled down the window. The November breeze hit her cheeks with cold. She felt the wind on her eyelids. Then she heard a scale. After waiting a few moments, she shut down the motor and opened the door. More sound came in. It touched her along her spine and danced in her veins. It skimmed along the tops of the red peaks and hung between the cliffs like a veil.

"That's beautiful, Michael," she breathed. "Really beautiful."

The distance from the car to the stoop had stretched into miles. Every step across the carpet of dead leaves was a heavy one, challenging her, harassing every motion of her body, striking her to the very core with a column of pain.

When the plaintive notes stopped, she knew he had sensed her coming. His shadow rose behind the curtain in the window, Ellen's white handiwork standing between them, as ephemeral as gauze.

The door opened. He stood with the bassoon still hanging from its strap around his neck, his long fingers on its keys. "Marissa?" His face was pale.

"Michael," she tried to say, but it came out more of a whisper.

"I couldn't figure out why they wanted you to stay in town just to sign papers." The canyon rang with the echo of the instrument. "Are you okay?"

She was not okay. Too much had passed since they had seen one another. He was leaving her with a responsibility she never dreamed she would dispatch by marrying the county recorder. And there were other pieces of a huge puzzle she would have to share with him.

"Michael, do you have a minute to talk?" A minute? An hour. Two hours. A lifetime.

"Sure. Come on in. We missed you." He held the door for her. He must have sensed something. "Did everything go okay?"

The room seemed darker than it had ever seemed in the morning. The shades were drawn. "Where's Joey?"

Michael paused. "He's in the orchard, mulching leaves." The dark room seemed to turn around them. "Is everything okay? Marissa . . . you . . . you seem troubled."

I am troubled, Michael. And you will soon be troubled too.

"Someone . . ." She tried to untie her tongue. There was so much, she didn't know where to begin. "Someone . . ." Now she suspected it was Wade Keller. He was the only person outside of the family who had known that Papa Bradley buried a box on the Watchman to save their most precious documents from the flood. "I think it was Wade Keller."

"What? What about Wade Keller? What?" Michael was in his chair now, the instrument draped across his lap. He released the reed from the mouthpiece and placed it in his mouth.

"Someone—and I'm pretty sure it was Wade Keller—went up to the Watchman without letting us know, found the box, and gave it to the courthouse."

Michael's mouth stayed frozen on the reed. "What?" He repeated the question as though he had not heard. "Wade Keller? I always wondered why we saw him so many times." Michael lowered his eyes.

"I just talked to him."

"Did he tell you this?"

"No. Never mind how I know. He helped me when my car ran out of gas. I believe he is the brother of one of the secretaries at the courthouse." But Marissa was rambling now. She needed to focus. "First, about the box. I need to talk to you."

Michael's look was penetrating. His eyes were wide with anticipation. Or fear.

"You are not on the will."

It was strange to behold his calm—as though no material thing in all the world could cut away the sinews of his soul. He did not blink, as if he were saying "So?"

"I saw a note from Mother explaining . . ." Here Marissa stammered, reaching for a possible way to prevent all of the painful truth from clattering out upon the air without shattering the windows of their souls. "Mother always knew you were not . . ."

Michael narrowed his eyes.

"Remember the baby she found in the pool of calm water against the crook of a tree?" Marissa finally asked. When she added, "You?" she felt the remorse of it crowd her speech. "You were . . . not her own baby. But . . ." Marissa could not say it. "Someone else's baby. Whose, no one will ever know for sure."

Michael did not move. His eyes were riveted to her lips. "What?" The room was so quiet Marissa could hear the thrash of Joey's rake in the yard, the buzz of the trucks and automobiles that moved up the road to the camp at the tunnel.

"Marissa," Michael said. "What . . . what? What are you saying to me?" He waited in the silence, she realized, because he knew what she was saying and it was swimming from a dark undertow to the surface of his brain. But he didn't want to see it yet. He would not look if he could help it. It was a wild revelation, stinging the air with some poison—a water moccasin, slippery and dark. He would try to skip away from it if he could, bury it before it came rushing to him with such force that it cracked his earth open and he would be compelled to look into the maw to see.

"Blair says—" Marissa began.

"Who's Blair?"

"The county recorder. He believes we should sell the farm to the government, and out of the funds . . . enough for your school . . ." She paused.

Michael was looking away from her now, as if the news had hit him so sharply it had thrust his head off kilter, and he was taking time to assimilate what he had heard. Marissa wondered if he was making connections with his past—why he was so different from the Rosefield boys, why he wanted music so much instead of cars, or money, or cantaloupes. Or peaches.

"I didn't want to tell you." Marissa swallowed hard.

"Unbelievable," Michael finally said. It came through his mouth, but it missed his voice.

The room seemed to tilt to the right and then to the left. Marissa had one more truth. "We were never brother and sister."

At this, Michael swung to face her. His eyes narrowed again as he took it in. "You mean . . ."

She nodded.

"All these years, I—" he started

"We were so careful. Yet . . ."

The unspoken words rang against the whitewashed walls and shook in the light.

In that moment Marissa felt she knew Michael's thoughts as she had never known them before. It seemed he was now aware of the meaning of everything that had ever passed between them: the heat, the pounding energy like auras of rainbows, the reaching, the swelling that surged into their instruments, the simmering when they had hit notes perfectly in tune, like a buzz in the ears, a hum, like muses moving through the paths of air.

"You mean . . ." He rose from what seemed like a stupor. He still sucked on the reed in his mouth. With the index finger on the hand that was not touching the keys, he pointed to himself, then to her. "You mean, we . . ." He lowered his eyes again, clearly unable to assimilate the shock. "Marissa, I'm . . ." He was searching for words. "I don't know what you are thinking . . ."

She did not know what she was thinking, or if there were even thoughts or wrinkles of thought that would ever come together.

Michael began to stammer, as though he understood what this news meant for both of them. "You . . . you know . . ."

What was it she was supposed to know?

He seemed to spit it out, weighed with confusion and bewilderment. "You realize I . . . I've made a commitment to Julie . . ."

Marissa knew. "Oh, of course," she babbled to cover the risk she had taken. "Oh no. Not that. I'm not . . . It's just that . . . you ought to know." She nodded slightly. But the tears began to stir again in her eyes. She knew he would not dishonor his commitments. He was as straight and ethical as anyone she had ever known. If there had at one time been a possibility for them to come together, that time had passed. "I know that, Michael. And I want you and Julie to be happy. And I'm . . ." Marissa was about to tell him she was married, but the words would not come yet. "You will go to Indiana and you will be very happy. You will have babies. And I will always love you." She paused. "But perhaps . . . just remembering . . . we might love one another more than just as brother and sister. Always. This will explain why I have fought so hard not to make more of our special friendship than we have already made—because I do love you, Michael, more than any person I can remember loving."

"Marissa . . ." he interrupted her. "You're wearing a gold band on your finger?"

There was the signal that she must bring the next truth to the dark room. There seemed to be more light now. The sun was seeping through the edges of the shade, through the lace of the white curtains. "I am married to the county recorder."

Michael's reaction was immediate and visible. He pulled back, and the reed rocked in his teeth. He took it out and held it in his fingers like a hot coal. So much had just hit him in a fury—like a conflagration burning out of control.

"No." The pause was deafening. "No. You're just saying . . ."

"No. It's true," she whispered. But she could not look into Michael's face. She looked down at the bassoon on his lap and wished for a fleeting moment that she was that bassoon cradled in his hands, so she could be held by him.

"Michael, please don't forget us," Marissa whispered. "Write to us from Indiana. Blair and I will live here at the farm with Joey until it is sold and we can get a house."

After a pause, Michael raised his eyes. "Is that his name? Blair?"

"Blair Harper. He's the country recorder. You know I was going in to the office more times than any of us believed possible. All this time we've . . ."

"Yes, I know," Michael said, as though not wishing to hear any more.

"We were married three days ago."

"Well then. We never had our chance."

These were the words that rang in her memory. If ever she allowed herself to remember, she still heard those words said with a tone of sorrow and poignancy that allowed her to know forever that if they had ever had a chance, she and Michael might have been together. But it would never happen now, though her heart broke like the toy music box she received one Christmas. Before she could play with it, it had fallen apart.

"We'll always be family, Michael."

But the muscles around his eyes tightened. "Julie . . ." he began. "If only Julie would . . ."

It was his truth now.

"She doesn't like me, does she?"

Michael's pause spoke volumes. "I've . . . I've praised you . . ."

Michael. Michael.

"Every time— I sometimes look for you in her, and I know it isn't fair. When I talk about you, she gets . . . upset."

Michael, Michael. Oh, please don't. "Michael, you mustn't. You mustn't talk about me. You must promise me never to compare us. It will hurt her feelings."

"I wanted us all to be friends. I wanted . . ."

Marissa had never been friends with Julie—the beautiful Julie who preferred her own family to the broken Rosefields. And when Marissa thought about it, she could remember some of Julie's comments about the Rosefields. "None of the Rosefield family went on missions, or went to college. We'll change that, won't we, Michael—especially about the college?" Tall, gorgeous Julie, daughter of Bishop Robinson, had looked down on the dirt in Morgan's and Carter's fingernails. Marissa remembered her saying, "The Rosefields are working people, but there is more to life than that." The moment Julie saw Michael, she had set her cap for him. She was a bright, laughing, enthusiastic, popular girl who always got what she wanted, and for some reason—perhaps because Michael had been comparing—she wanted to take him away forever. And it looked like it was going to happen, didn't it? Marissa would lose so much this year: Mother, Papa, Morgan, Carter, the farm—almost all of her life. And Michael . . .

She still had Joey. At that moment, she heard a slam in the shed, a rustle, and then footsteps. Joey came through the door.

Marissa smiled to see him. He was so tall now, his shoulders so broad. The pools of his blue eyes seemed deep.

"Marissa!" He smiled. "We wondered why you had to stay overnight just to sign some papers."

"She's married," Michael said. "They kept it secret."

"Married?"

Marissa held out her hand with the ring. "I'm Mrs. Harper now." She tried to smile, but the weight of everything had crippled her face.

"You're joking!"

"No. It's true. I married the county recorder, Blair Harper. Just a few days ago. He will live here with us until we sell the farm."

Joey took her fingers in his and looked at the ring. "Looks like a wedding band. Is it gold?"

Marissa laughed. *Who knows?* It was ironic. She really *didn't* know. "If it turns my finger green, I s'pose it isn't."

"Wow! Who woulda guessed you'd go off behind our backs and get married?"

Well, it wasn't exactly like that, was it?

"We were going to tell you. I'm telling you now," Marissa stammered. "I know Michael and Julie are planning a big party at Christmastime. But Blair is a private person." Pain stabbed through Marissa. Just how private was he? she wondered. "He didn't want that much fuss. And, well . . ." She hesitated. "He isn't a member of the Church." She paused. "But he . . . has a good job. He's a nice man. And I'll bring him to meet you very soon."

"Yeah. He must be a sneak to run off with the only girl in the Rosefield family," Joey said. "Probably looks like a gorilla."

Marissa laughed. "No such thing. He has your color of hair. And yes, he sort of reminds me of you."

Michael finally spoke. "We just want the best for all of us." His voice sounded distant, as though he were including all the world.

Joey went to the kitchen sink and washed his hands.

Twenty

When Marissa opened the door to the basement apartment, she found Blair sitting on the side of the bed with his elbows on his knees, his hands covering his face.

"Are you all right?" she asked.

He opened one hand and gazed at her. "It took you that long? Where have you been all this time?"

"If you've been asleep . . ." She hesitated. "Does it matter?"

He swore again. "Don't argue with me."

"I wasn't arguing. I just wanted to know—"

"Shut up!" he screamed. "I can't believe this. You wake me up at four in the morning and I'm so wide awake I didn't get back to sleep until just a couple of hours ago. Then you clatter in. You robbed me of sleep, and then you want to argue with me."

"I'm sorry." She was sorry. The pain of all she had gone through this morning was still clinging to her. "Why are you so upset now? You were all right at the motel. This is the first I've seen you like this."

The expression on his face changed. "All right, Marissa. You're right. I'm sorry. I didn't mean to explode like that. I missed you. Come on, don't look at me like that."

She didn't know how she was feeding his anger.

"How did it go?" Blair asked.

"I ran out of gas."

"What?" He squinted when he looked at her now.

"Wade Keller helped me." She went to the dresser to pull out the drawer, put away her scarf. "I didn't know Wade and Bruzy were brother and sister."

"Oh?" Blair seemed far away, inaccessible, in some kind of fog. "Yeah. They came out from New York."

"Was it Wade who brought you the box from the Watchman?"

For a moment the room seemed to spin.

"Huh?" Blair got up from the bed.

"Why didn't you tell us? It was our box."

"I don't think he knew whose box it was."

"He knew," Marissa said. "He got it off the Watchman. That's on the corner of our farm. He was there when Papa Bradley died."

"Well, it would have come out that Michael wasn't part of the family anyway. He wasn't on the legal records in the files, either."

"He wasn't?"

"No."

"Why didn't you tell me sooner?"

"Look, Marissa, we did the best we could. We were surprised to find Ellen's note that confused the problem. How did he take it, anyway?" Blair looked up at her, but his eyes stayed in a squint.

"He isn't that kind of person."

"What do you mean?"

"He doesn't care about money. He just wants to play music and to help others enjoy music."

Something not right moved around the room, like a spirit of digression hovering in the corners and playing havoc with the air.

"Put your scarf back on. Let's go get something to eat," Blair said. "I'm sorry I got all bent out of shape."

"You knew Michael wasn't . . ." She couldn't seem to let it go.

"Let's go. Come on."

If she had known sooner, would it have made any difference? Marissa wasn't sure.

When they got to the café, Rosie grinned at them before she took her pencil down from her ear. "You two are lookin' cozy. What's goin' on?"

"We're married, Rosie," Blair said.

She picked up Marissa's hand and fingered the ring. "Whoop de doo! Whyn't you tell me? I woulda got out a rubber band! When did this happen?"

"Couple days ago." Blair smiled. "We've been on a honeymoon."

"Wow! I thought . . ." Rosie was savvy. She had started something, and she puzzled it through with a little humor. "Well, bozo! What happened to the blond?"

"Who, Bruzy? She still works for me."

"Oh, you don't say? What kin' a work?"

"Secretarial work, Rosie. Typing, filing. You knew that," he almost growled.

"You get 'em, dump 'em." She grinned. "This one's for keeps?"

"This one's for keeps." Blair reached for Marissa's hand.

"Well, I'm glad to see you finally settled down," Rosie said.

Blair smiled. "We're till death do us part."

He ordered a steak sandwich with cheese, the most expensive item on the menu. "Go ahead," he told Marissa. "Splurge. When we sell out, we're gonna have enough money to go to the moon."

Something wrong was still settling in Marissa's chest, something she was not familiar with. *What happened to the blond?* The cloud that obscured her vision came down again. When the food arrived, she happened to glance out the window and saw two men coming up the walk. They pounded the pavement forcefully, as if they were not in pursuit of a steak sandwich, but had some urgent business. When the door opened, she felt a blast of cold air at her feet.

"We're looking for Blair Harper," the leading man said.

Rosie didn't pause, concentrating on the platter in her hands. She pointed to the corner where the newlyweds sat. "Lover boy and his new wife," she said. Her words carried to everyone in the café. Some heads came up.

Marissa froze. *What now?*

The men walked over. "Blair Harper?"

He had a bite of steak in his mouth but got out a muffled "Yeah?"

"We need to talk to you."

Suddenly, Blair had his charming face on. "Talk," he said. "Want a bite of steak sandwich? It's pretty tasty."

"No, thank you," one of the men replied. "We need you to come with us."

"Hey! You wanna interrupt a man's dinner? The lady told ya . . ." He tossed his head toward Rosie. "We're newlyweds. This is our honeymoon. Come on! Move over, Marissa. Let the gentlemen sit down. We'll share with ya."

Marissa moved.

"No. Come on, Mr. Harper. Not here. At the police station."

Her heart fell. Something was very wrong.

For a moment there was a silent tug of war. Blair did not get up. He did not react. His eyes were frozen in a silly stare, while his jaw continued to chomp on the steak sandwich.

"You can bring your sandwich with you," the second man said in a voice that sounded high and squeaky, like a girl's. He was dressed in a black pea coat that fell to his knees, and he wore a Scotch-plaid tie.

The leader of the two men was chunkier, with a pair of glasses on a chain around his neck. "Sorry, Mr. Harper, we don't want to interrupt no honeymoon. But we need to ask you a few questions, and we don't got much time."

"Well, I'm not goin' anywhere without my bride," Blair said, his mouth now full. "Rosie, box it up!"

By the time she had boxed it up, the lawmen were nervous as two cats in a pit. They wouldn't let Blair take his car. They gave blunt directions. "Well, both of you sit in the back, then. You can play lovey-dovey, but the honeymoon might be over."

Marissa didn't look out of the car windows to see where they were going. She lowered her eyes, hoping to delay learning what this was all about. In the last few blocks to the police station she closed her eyes. She prayed silently. *Dear God, please help us. Please, whatever this is. Please.*

She didn't know Blair was watching her. "Say a prayer for me too, Marissa," he mumbled.

She didn't know how he found her out. She glanced at him. His eyes were full of fire.

At the police station, they sat around a table in a small, sterile room. The leading detective put his glasses on his nose. "You must know what this is all about."

Blair seemed in a state of stupor, as though he were drunk. "Ha! No! I haven't the foggiest idea in the world what you all brought us here for."

"We brought in a Wade Keller. Do you know a Wade Keller?"

"Wade Keller?" A light flickered behind Blair's eyes. "Well . . . why should I know Wade Keller?"

The little man with the big glasses took off his coat. The stove in the other room was belching, even though it was just November and still warm there in St. George. "You gonna tell the truth, or you gonna hedge and make it worse?" he squeaked in his little-girl voice.

"No. I . . . I'll tell the truth. Why shouldn't I tell the truth?"

Marissa heard something in Blair's voice she wanted to question, a kind of pain. He was nervous, she could tell, like a worm pinned to the ground with a toothpick.

"I'm just asking . . . why should you be asking me if I know a Wade Keller?"

"We took him in today," the lead detective said.

For a moment the room was quiet. Blair was quiet. The crackle of the unnecessary fire in the front-room stove made a tense background fracas, an appropriate accompaniment of noisy heat.

Even Marissa began to sweat. But she did not take off her coat. She did not move.

"Tell us what you know about Wade Keller."

Blair tried laughing, a very weak one that ended too abruptly. "He's from New York."

"And his sister?"

"Well . . ." Blair was still reluctant, still hedging. "Yeah. He has a sister." He paused. The room seemed to be getting cloudy. "Lots of people have sisters." He drummed his fingers on the table. "So what do you want to know about his sister?"

"Her name. Her occupation?"

"Yeah." It was obvious Blair sensed he wasn't telling them anything they didn't know. He was playing their game. "Bruzy Keller. She works with me in the county recorder's office."

The head detective, whose name was on his badge—George Canby—rifled through some papers in a folder and began writing on one of the blank forms. "We might as well tell you, Mr. Harper, a man named Bertie Smith who works for the post office in the Springdale grocery store called us this morning. A certain package came in for a Mr. Wade Keller, but it wasn't the first time such a package came in for Mr. Keller."

Blair tried to look nonchalant, but he slipped his fingers off the table and hid them in his lap. His hands visibly shook.

"He got away with it once, he thought. And we suspect he thought he could get away with it again." Canby paused.

"Get away with what?" Blair's voice was small.

"We think you know," the squeaky detective told him.

For the first time Blair did not answer. He kept his hands under the table.

"Don't you want to know what was in the package?" Canby asked.

Blair did not answer.

"Bertie Smith thought he knew, so he called us to investigate."

Why? Marissa wondered. Everything that had happened today began to spin like the rocks in the kaleidoscopes they sold as trinkets to park visitors. She felt numb, as though everything plunging into the abyss of her life were those sharp rocks hitting her, tearing her on the way down. What had happened? She was afraid she was going to find out.

"You knew, didn't you, Mr. Harper?" Canby asked. "You knew what was in the package."

Blair did not move. But his eyes clouded over, and his lips twitched.

"It's been a few weeks. But I guess you might have heard we found explosives residue in the wreckage of the accident that killed Morgan and Carter Rosefield. Wade told us . . ."

Blair's lips started turning blue.

Marissa took a deep breath. *No! No!*

Finally Blair spoke. His voice was low, as though it came from somewhere deep. "I had nothin' to do with it. You can't find any proof I had anything to do with it."

Canby pushed his glasses back on his nose. "With what, Mr. Harper?"

"With Wade's . . ." He was digging himself deeper.

"That's not what Mr. Keller tells us."

Oh no! Marissa felt a stinging in her head she had never felt before. Her senses reeled. Blair and Wade. And probably Bruzy. What had happened was dropping down on her like a huge cloud—one so thick the air felt like water. She felt her stomach twist as though it would soon wring the very life out of her.

"We know what relationship you have with Bruzy." Squeaky grinned.

"Thought you'd get away with a tidy marriage, sell the property . . ." Canby continued.

Marissa saw stars, the kind she got from shutting her eyes after looking at bright lights. Lights that make everything clear. Is that where Blair went on their wedding night—to Bruzy? Marissa's dreams—the imagined scenarios of a marriage with the handsome county recorder—suddenly collapsed like the corrugated edges of a cardboard box left out in the rain. She glanced at Blair. He seemed so small now. He was curled up at the table, his hands still hidden. He had leaned forward, his upper arms pressed against the edge—almost as though he would gladly saw his body in half at that moment, press himself into pieces that might end whatever was about to come to him.

"We have enough evidence to book you now," Squeaky said.

"You don't have proof of nothing," Blair murmured. But everything about his body made things very clear.

"Mrs. Harper can go now."

Marissa could go? Where? Back to nothing. There would be nothing. Blair would be going to jail. There would be an annulment. Or a divorce. She faded in and out of terrible visions—of Wade packing the truck with explosives, of the fire suddenly blossoming on the road, eating her brothers alive. She knew in her heart of hearts that Bruzy had been in on it. But what Marissa did not know for sure was the purpose of the second box of explosives. She shuddered at the realization that it might have been for her.

She realized she wasn't breathing. She sucked at the air.

"I'll take you back to the café, or to Blair's. He won't be needing his place anymore, I can vouch for that," Squeaky told her. "Got another place to stay?"

Barely. Her heart was like a wild animal batting against her rib cage. The ride to the café was punctuated by Mr. Squeaky's profoundly expert analysis of everything that had transpired in the last two months. Marissa was relieved to get out at Rosie's Café, but she didn't go in. She slumped in Blair's car and waited to find some semblance of sanity. Finally, she inserted the key, turned it, and started the engine.

What would Michael say now? Marissa bent over the steering wheel and drove as though she were in a stupor. It had happened so fast—like the rapid-shutter-quick scenes of a bad movie with Greta Garbo she had once seen. *Clap clap clap*. The images ratcheted by so quickly it gave the illusion of a film. This scene was Marissa's, and it wasn't pretty. It was tragic. She had fallen for a liar. And though she had guessed he had been acting all this time, she had not wanted it to be true.

Nothing. Nothing. She had nothing. She didn't want to go back to Michael and beg. How distasteful it would be to her. But he would discover all of this soon. It would be in the paper. It would be on Bertie Smith's lips. The boxes of Marissa's life had enclosed her. She felt trapped, anchorless.

Yet, there was the critical legal record—that she alone was now the owner of the Rosefield property. It meant, first, that she could procure the loan against it to send Michael to school. She would sacrifice everything for the brother she loved more than life itself. If he was not her "real" brother, he was the love of her life. And she would see that everything he worked for would bring him joy.

And she still had Joey to care for. He was still a boy. She would give him everything he needed to become an upright, honorable man.

Twenty-one

It didn't hit her at first—what had overcome her in those moments in the hot room at the police station. But after a few days when something heavy began to push at her in her breasts, she knew. She was pregnant.

She stayed at the empty apartment for a few days because she did not want to interrupt Michael's work at the camp. She did not want to face Joey with the entire travesty. Not yet. She felt lost, unhinged, off balance. But deep in her heart she was smiling. No, it wasn't the best of circumstances. The father of her child was perhaps not the father she would have chosen—if she could have chosen. But it would be a beautiful child, and it would be hers.

The light over the red cliffs seemed rosy to her. The days were still mild, and gold leaves still hung on some of the trees.

Marissa spent her time walking. She walked up into the red hills. She bought groceries and cooked meals she liked: spare ribs with sweet potatoes and green beans, spaghetti with tomato sauce and grated cheddar cheese.

She did not go back to the jail. She did not see Blair. She did not check to see if anyone came to get him out on a bond. He must have been trying to contact the government to get him out, but even if he was successful, Marissa would be gone. She waited until Friday to pack, and she drove in the evening to the farm, when she knew Michael would be back from the camp.

The lights in the house were bright, and again she could hear the pure, clear sound of the bassoon playing against the Steamboat Mountain and the Patriarchs, still standing firm as they had always stood. And would stand, long after she and Michael and Joey—even her child—were gone forever. These rocks were more forever than human life, a reminder to anyone who looked at them in awe that those who played around them and loved them were gone, and would leave others to gaze in wonder at the Zion that would never die.

When the motor stopped, Marissa waited a moment to gather her courage. It was obvious Michael was there. And Joey would probably be there. She saw the second car of Bishop Robinson's family—a little gray coupe with a bulging trunk. Michael must have been offered the car to drive back and forth to work. It was generous of them to lend it to him when the truck was destroyed. The old Chevy, so unreliable, cowered behind the barn as though it had been put into a hospital.

Marissa reached the door but stopped before she knocked, because she was hearing a piece she knew, and she did not want to interrupt. The magic of Schubert's "Pastorale" pealed through the cool November air with a wave of sadness.

After she knocked, she heard the last few measures again. But someone was coming to the door, for she heard footsteps. *It must be Joey.*

But it was not Joey. The door opened only slightly, and a beautiful, pale face appeared, framed in dark curls.

"Oh, hello, Julie," Marissa said. "How are you?" *Julie.* This classic face would belong to her family someday.

An arctic wind blew against the Watchman and rippled through the orchard to the front door.

"Hi, Marissa." But Julie did not open the door. She held it against the cold, against the evening falling fast around them.

Marissa was taken aback and could not seem to breach the cold, the wind sounding now like a squall in her ears. "Are . . . are my brothers here?"

"Yes," Julie said tentatively. "Michael's practicing."

Yes. Marissa could hear him, of course. "I . . . I . . ." she began.

"Michael told me you got married. It was a surprise to all of us," Julie said it through the crack in the door. Marissa heard it ring with the slight edge of contempt. Of course, Julie's very circumspect bishop's family would have looked upon the sister of their new son-in-law, if not with disdain, with concern—with questions, perhaps wondering if this was, after all, the family Julie should have chosen to join.

"Yes, yes, I did. But—"

"He doesn't want to be interrupted."

"Is Joey here?"

"No. He's on a date."

Joey was on a date? He had just turned sixteen.

There wasn't enough warmth from the house to neutralize the cold Marissa felt at both her front and her back. This was her home. Or was it anymore? "May I . . . may I come in?"

Michael didn't want to be interrupted.

Marissa heard a phrase from the "Pastorale" that he was repeating, repeating. She knew the strings beneath her fingers so well, they sang to her memory. She would have joined him if she could. Could Julie truly keep her out? She couldn't believe it. She was still standing in the cold. But she would do it no longer. So she reached out for the door. Julie backed away when Marissa opened the screen. "I'll be quiet," she said and pushed her way in.

Michael's back was to her. He was sitting on the piano bench facing the piano.

"Oh!" He turned to see her, and his eyes narrowed in the light. "Marissa!"

It was in his voice—his surprise, and his love. "What are you doing here? I didn't expect you . . ." He turned on the bench and laid the bassoon on his lap.

"Michael!" She swallowed everything she wanted to tell him. "Joey went on a date?" She glanced at Julie. The beautiful face was frozen in what looked like fear, or anger. "How did that happen?"

Michael smiled. "Remember Morgan and Wade's girlfriend, Maxine? Her younger sister."

"Pam?" Marissa knew her as a child with freckles and pigtails.

"She broke her leg stepping in a ditch. Joey walked her home from school every day, with the cast on her leg. Her parents agreed to drive them to the movies."

Marissa smiled, picturing sweet Joey being compassionate. "That's great. Things are happening so fast." There was a drafty pause. She had come in upon them, and the air was singing, but was it with the "Pastorale," or a nervous energy she could not recognize? She would put them at ease. "And now you're busy getting ready for that wedding." She looked at Julie and smiled, consciously bringing warmth to her voice.

Julie did not smile back.

"I'd like to help wherever I can . . ." Marissa said, but Julie did not move. "At least with the refreshments. Have you planned what you'll serve? It's in the recreation hall, I trust?"

Michael rescued Julie from the silence. "That would be so nice of you, Marissa. Thank you. Sister Robinson is in charge of that. You can offer her your help."

Marissa had already spoken to Sister Robinson. The Robinsons were passing Marissa back and forth from one to another like a kick ball.

“What are you having?” She was almost on the edge of not trying anymore, but she wanted so much to love Julie and be a part of their lives. Everything Marissa had ever loved the best was wrapped into this package.

“Oh, probably fruit compote,” Julie said at last.

“They’ll use some cantaloupes.” Michael grinned. “Think we can get some of those somewhere?”

She smiled because he was joking with her. There were still plenty of cantaloupes in the field. In this mild climate, they would stay good on the vines until December.

There was a moment of silence. Nothing. No words. No bassoon.

“Julie, I want to be your friend. I want to help you. You and Michael will be going away soon.”

“You’re not related to him.” Julie’s words crashed through the silence like explosions.

Marissa looked at Michael. “You told her.”

His face colored. He was caught between two people he loved, and it was closing in on him like a vice. “She had a right to know I wasn’t in the will.”

“But Julie . . .” She turned to the beautiful girl. She was beautiful. She would make beautiful children. She lowered her eyes, and a thick row of dark lashes lay on her cheeks. “Julie, didn’t Michael tell you I am planning on funding his schooling?”

“I know.”

Michael got up from the piano bench. He laid the bassoon on the floor and came to stand by his fiancée, putting his arm around her shoulders. “She’s upset. You would . . .” He looked in Julie’s eyes. There was love in his face—caring, a shelter for a young woman who was totally smitten, and he would not hurt her. “She was worried . . . you would be in charge.”

Marissa’s heart knocked against her ribs.

"She doesn't know you, Marissa." He paused. "So she doesn't—"

"Trust me," Marissa finished. "But Julie, I was hoping you would . . ." She could feel tears coming, but she shook them off. "We need to be good friends."

"We're your friends, Marissa." Michael held Julie close and glanced to Marissa. "We're willing to be good friends."

The pause was pregnant.

"We don't know your husband." Julie looked up at Michael. Her gaze was absorbing. "Maybe *you'll* want to help us. But we don't know about him."

Marissa's mind spun. They were still standing. Not even Michael had invited Marissa to sit down. It became clear to her that she was intruding. There was an undeniable pulse of fire that danced over Michael and Julie. Marissa knew what it was, for she had felt it with him. And she had felt it at one time with Blair. It was strong. She wanted to break through the light, to tell them how she felt, to fall at Michael's feet and sob for her need. But she loved him so much she could not. And what would she tell them? Legally, she was still married. The news would be . . . damaging? Obsolete? Too late? Perhaps it would be better if they learned everything from some other source. She was sensitive enough to realize she was being shut out.

Michael and Julie stood together, believing Marissa was still married. And she was.

"I'm sorry I bothered you. I just wanted to drop by for a visit. I should have called first . . ."

"No, no," Michael protested. "Anytime, Marissa. You don't need to call. Just come . . ." When he paused, the silence seemed ominous.

"No, I'll be going," Marissa stammered. "You two have a wonderful evening."

She barely got out of the house graciously before she broke down and sobbed. She did not go back to the car. She walked toward the barn. Her barn. The irony of it hit her with a force she hadn't expected. She felt homeless in her own home. She had no place to lay her head.

The wind had died down. The canyon was suspended in a kind of buzz. Or was it just in her mind? She heard the mew of a barn cat somewhere, the snort of Joey's horse in the stable. The moon was just waning from its full harvest glow. The trees were still hanging with dry leaves. She walked toward the orchard, sucking up her tears, wiping her cheeks with her hands. *Heavenly Father, what have I done? What is happening to me? How could I have been so mistaken about Blair?* She still loved the man she had imagined he was. She had an imagination, all right. She could never go back to him now. He had betrayed her. Completely. There was reason to believe he and Bruzy and Wade had planned . . .

For a moment Marissa couldn't breathe. She consciously told herself to take a breath of air. *Please, Heavenly Father, be with me. Guide me. Hold me. I need help . . . to get through all of this. So much. So much.*

In the distance she could hear what sounded like the howl of a coyote. Let the canyon cry out Marissa's distress. There was room enough in the yard for the explosion in her heart, the implosion of her losses. The magnificence of the canyon walls rang back to her like the sound of village bells. *Oh, dear Father, this is the time I must search for your answers. The world seems to be turning away from me. I am so deep in a sorrow I cannot fathom. Where do I belong? Where do I fit in all of this? And I will probably be a mother soon! The greatest responsibility I could ever have imagined. And I know . . . I know it will take all of my life to dispatch this duty with love, with courage, with the knowledge of how vastly important it is to bring a life into this world that will add to, not detract from, mankind's joy.*

Marissa walked. She took the path through the orchard to the field of cantaloupes. And to the Watchman, where her father had buried the critical information that, if it had been available earlier, may have altered her entire life.

But she knew she could not play those kinds of thoughts in her head. It would be unproductive. Life gave you what it gave you—the parents it gave you, the place of your childhood, the friends who came across your path. You made decisions in relationship to those factors. If you wanted happiness and peace, you looked for ways you could make those around you feel joy so that their joy would buoy you up in hard times. There were no guarantees in life. Life was not always fair. But learning to make the best of things would make it worthwhile.

What should she do?

She would take out a loan on the property, and with some of it she would support Michael's schooling. And with the rest, she would go to Salt Lake City and find Uncle Peter and Aunt Sophie, ask them if they could keep her until she could get an apartment, have this baby, love this child with all of her heart—love it so much she would teach it to be good. If there was anything in Blair's makeup to cast a deceitful, lax spirit upon this child, Marissa would work so hard to change that tendency. She would do anything in her power to bring a child into the world who would be strong, one that would hold fast to the commandments.

At the edge of the orchard she heard a motor on the road and realized a car had stopped at the house. A flurry of doors opening and closing caught her attention.

Joey. It would be about time for the end of his movie. Maxine's parents would be letting him off after he said goodbye to the little sister, Pam.

On her way back to the house, Marissa heard the motor of the Robinsons' car spin into a full-throttled hum. Julie would be driving away.

Still feeling all of the hurt, the tragedy of her life bearing down upon her heart, Marissa quickened her step to the door. She knew Michael and Joey would welcome her to the home she had always known, embrace her in the memory of their mother and their father, present to her reminders of their sweet faces and open arms. They would listen to her and love her—with the same love that echoed in these canyon walls with the music of their dreams. The love that bore them up always. They were family. And the peace that was always with them would be with them always.

Joey could keep the farm. Someday, if they were forced to sell the canyon property, they would have enough to make a new start.

When she entered the house, Michael was in his room with the door shut. Joey was at the kitchen sink, washing and drying a few pots and pans and stashing them under the curtain that hung over the lower shelves Bradley had built for Ellen so many years ago. It seemed like an eternity had passed since their voices had softly echoed through the house.

"Did you have fun?"

"Oh, Marissa." Joey turned but kept his hands in the dishwater. "I didn't know you were home."

"Do you like her?"

He stopped for a moment, his eyes searching his sister's. "Yes, very much. I wish I was older than sixteen."

"There's time." Marissa smiled. "Be patient."

Joey must have sensed something beneath the smile. "What are you doing here? Where is your husband?"

In halting phrases she told him everything—except that she believed she was going to have a baby.

He dropped all that was left from the sink into the pan he was using to wash dishes, and stopped and turned fully toward her. "Marissa! No!" His face grew pale. "I wondered why Wade was always . . . And Morgan and Carter. No, no!"

"Please don't tell Michael," she whispered. "I don't want him to worry. He has his future . . ."

"Ha!" Joey faced the sink again. "That news will get out so fast. Probably already is. You can't . . . What makes you think you can keep it from Michael?"

"Please, Joey. Michael knows I'm married to Blair. But he doesn't know about the arrests. Wait to tell him. At least until he finds something out on his own and the wedding is over. If he asks me questions, I'll answer them. Please tell him I am just here to . . . go to church on weekends. And to help with the wedding."

She woke at dawn because she heard a car in the driveway. When she pushed aside the curtain over the window in her room, she saw it was Julie.

"We're going hiking in Grand Canyon," she heard Michael call to Joey from the door. Michael didn't know Marissa was lurking in the background. It was just as well.

When Joey came in from milking, she cooked him breakfast.

"That's new," he said. "We've been batchin' for so long." He washed his hands in the sink, then used his fingers to take a lump of scrambled eggs from the frying pan. "I'm glad. Not about the terrible things that have happened. But I'm glad you'll be here with us. You can help me run the farm."

Michael came home so late in the evening that Marissa didn't see him. He was spinning in a different orbit, and it wasn't hers.

She was almost asleep, but she heard him meet Joey on the way out of the bathroom.

"Did Marissa leave some of her things in the bathroom?" he asked Joey.

"Yeah. She's staying here a couple of nights on the weekend to help with the wedding."

On Sunday, Michael could not help but see her. "You going to church with us?" he asked her.

"Remember, I told you . . . Blair isn't a member."

Michael accepted that answer without further explanation.

"You going with Joey, or do you want to ride with us? Julie is coming to pick me up."

Marissa did a double take. "I don't think Julie would want me to ride with you."

Michael was shaving his neck, looking sidelong into the mirror. But at Marissa's hesitant comment, he glanced at her. "No, it would be . . ." He stopped. "Maybe you're right." He didn't speak for a moment, but neither did she. There was an emptiness that seemed alive, begging for something to fill it up. "We'll need to be patient with her. Ever since the news about the farm—my not being . . ."

"I know, Michael. Please don't worry about it. I completely understand."

He was out the door in a moment when the Robinsons came.

Joey drove the Chevrolet to church. Marissa kept from answering questions or speaking in any of the meetings. Sunday dinner without Michael seemed empty, but she was glad he wasn't there. Supper was leftover stew, and Joey was riveted to the newspaper while he ate. Marissa waited nervously for an outburst at some tidbit of information he might catch about what was going on behind the scenes. But it did not happen. If the city desk had heard anything at all, they had evidently considered it inconsequential. There was nothing in the newspaper about Blair's arrest.

When Michael left for camp in the morning, still nothing had been said.

Twenty-two

It was Wednesday when the sheriff came. Marissa was not ready for this. After helping Joey gather eggs, her hair was a frizz, escaping a hasty bandana. When the police car drove up, she was washing the eggs at the outdoor pump.

The sheriff did not get out of his car immediately, as though waiting to make sure he was at the right spot. And when he opened the door, her heart skipped a beat. When he came around to the passenger side and opened the back door, a shock rippled through her. It was Blair. He climbed out of the back seat of the car, feet first. He pushed at the door to stand up, as though he had been cramped in the cell for so long, he couldn't walk.

For a moment everything froze for her: the image of the sheriff dangling his keys at his belt, the sun filtering through the red light on the roof of the police vehicle, the trees stripped of their leaves, the patriarchal red monoliths leaning over everything as though on an investigation of their own.

Blair may have seemed cramped, but he had some kind of confidence inherent in his swagger, one Marissa guessed would never go away. He moved toward her with the look in his eyes she had come to know the past five months—his charming, persuasive self.

"Marissa!" His tone was like honey.

"He's come to get his car," the sheriff said. "Do you have the keys?"

The keys were on the little table by the door in Aunt Sophie's Christmas candy dish.

"Yes. I'll get the keys."

Blair tried to follow her into the house.

"Please," she called to the sheriff, "I'll bring them out!"

"All right, Harper. Just hang onto your horses," he said to Blair.

Once in the house, Marissa looked out the window. She couldn't believe it. Blair. He looked desperate. His hair practically stood on end. He looked gaunt.

When she reached the men in the yard, she had Blair's car keys in her hand. He stepped toward her with urgency and then glanced at the officer. "Can you leave us alone for a few minutes?"

"Sure. But don't take long." The sheriff walked back to the vehicle with the red light and got in.

For a moment the silence hovered in the air. Then Blair said, "A friend in New York posted all of our bail."

"Oh." Marissa barely opened her mouth.

"Marissa! You've got to believe me. This is all cooked up out of nothing. It's a crazy lie." He began to speak faster. She felt a cold grip of nerves on her scalp.

"Wade asked Morgan and Carter if he could transport a load of dynamite with the cantaloupes. You've got to listen to me. He ordered it for a construction project on the new road in Bloomington. They said yes and put it in a box in the truck with their cantaloupes."

Morgan and Carter were dead. They would not back up the story. The people in charge of the construction project might know the truth.

Marissa waited for what seemed like forever. She did not feel like speaking.

"Wade is a liar. He hates me because of Bruzy . . ." Blair hesitated as though he had said too much.

Marissa wasn't able to stop the next words that rolled out of her mouth. "What about Bruzy. You were . . . like . . . married to her, weren't you?"

Blair moved closer. Marissa felt a kind of suffocation.

"No. No, I swear. I married you." He moved even closer. She shuddered.

"Come on, Marissa. You Mormons and your polygamy—you're acquainted with all of this kind of stuff. And I swear . . ."

"We don't do that any more, Blair," she said without feeling. "It's grounds to be excommunicated."

Of course he knew that. His eyes betrayed him. "There's no polygamy," he choked out, milking it for all it was worth. "I married you. And I need you, Marissa. Now more than ever. You think you're something special, a good *Mormon*. How could you make such a commitment and then . . . abandon it . . ." He stopped for a moment as if trying to collect himself. "I swear. It will come out in court, Marissa."

"About you and Bruzy?"

"All right." He backed off. "I was going with Bruzy. She wanted . . . she . . ."

"She wanted to marry you."

Blair stood over Marissa now, and though she tried to back away, he grasped her elbows. "Yes. But I'm in love with you."

Yes. And you're also in love with the money that will come from the property when and if it sells.

Marissa flinched, pulling away from him.

Blair's gaze narrowed as brilliant sunlight poured over the Watchman. He shielded his eyes. "Won't you listen to me? I was going with Bruzy. But when I saw you . . ." He paused. "Can't you believe me?"

She looked off in the distance at the police car and the red light catching the sun. "I don't feel particularly special."

He moved into the direct line of her vision. "Listen to me, Marissa." That had been the problem all along—the smooth voice, the bright eyes. The mellifluous tones reminded her of why she had been so persuaded.

"It's all going to go away. I promise you."

"What's going away?" she asked.

"This ridiculous charge of murder. It was all an accident." Blair paused, moving close to her. The power of his physical presence still made rivers rush in her blood. "Marissa, please."

But she couldn't speak. She should have guessed what Bruzy had meant to him, but her passion had blinded her.

"Get in the car with me. It will all come out in court. I swear I am innocent. Can't you get your things . . ."

She had to admit her heart was torn.

"Come here. I love you, Marissa. We can make a life together. You made a commitment to me. Aren't you going to honor that commitment?"

Still, she did not speak.

"Marissa! Speak to me." He swore. His tone suddenly changed. "Oh my gosh, look at you! The little *Mormon* girl who thinks she's so perfect, yet she can't even keep a commitment . . ."

She backed away from him. "Blair. Blair!"

"Blair, Blair!" He mocked her. "What in the heck do you think you're doing to me?" He swore again. He turned around and hit his palm with his fist. "Oh my gosh! How did this happen?" He turned back. "What do you want . . . a divorce?"

The sheriff got out of his car. He stood at the door, watching through the red light caught with the sun, blazing like a red fire.

"Blair, I'm sorry," she said. She raised his keys.

He looked at her for only an instant before he swiped the keys out of her hand.

The sheriff came to the front of the vehicle. "Sorry, Mrs. Harper. You ready to go now, Mr. Harper?" He moved like an officer moves sometimes, from one foot to the other, filling his chest with an authoritative breath.

Blair stomped toward the barn where his car was parked. Marissa's fear left her with each step. He was a spoiled child who had not gotten his way.

The sheriff followed him as he drove down the drive.

When Joey came in from the barn, he said, "I just heard a car drive away."

"Blair came and got his car," Marissa explained.

"Oh." Joey looked down the road. "Well, you know that scab that was on the cow's left rear foot? It came off. She's okay now."

The day of the wedding came amid a flurry of Christmas activities. Michael played "What Child Is This?" for the ward Christmas party on December 19th. Joey danced the entire evening with Maxine's sister, Pam. Marissa stayed in the background, serving the red Jell-O dessert with whipped cream.

On the twenty-third, the Robinsons picked up Michael early. Joey was too young to get a temple recommend, and Marissa did not have one. Neither of them would be able to attend the sealing ceremony in the St. George Temple. But both of them went to the recreation hall at the church and set up the tables.

Michael had dressed at the Robinsons' house. When the bride and groom came into the hall, both of their faces were flushed with the joy of the occasion. In the reception line, Michael held Marissa so close she trembled. "It was beautiful," he whispered. "I wish you could have been there."

Afterward, when he held her at arms' length, he said, "I haven't met your husband yet, Marissa. He was invited. I'd like to meet him sometime."

She ignored his comment. "I'm so happy for you, Michael." She reached out to Julie, who gave her a weak hand. "You look beautiful, Julie."

But Julie's tongue seemed to be in a knot.

"We're family now," Marissa said uneasily. Her words seemed to stick in her throat.

Julie's face could not have been more wooden. Was it fear behind her eyes, or was it shock? Some pain definitely lurked there. "It was a nice ceremony." Julie forced her words with a smile.

Brother and Sister Robinson were kind. They shook Marissa's hand warmly. "We're glad you could help us this afternoon," Mrs. Robinson said. "We wish you could have come to the temple . . . The bishop and I will have to meet your husband soon. Invite him to Church, won't you, one of these days?"

Blair was still very much on Marissa's mind. She bought every newspaper and combed it carefully. One Sunday before the wedding, a small paragraph announced that three fugitives had jumped bail. The suspicion was that they were driving to New York, but no one had apprehended them. Only Blair's name was included. When she saw the story, she gulped. But there was so much going on in the ward that the plans for the wedding and reception must have kept everyone she knew from reading the newspaper. It seemed impossible. But it was true. No one recognized the name Harper. They might have recognized Wade, but both he and Bruzy Keller seemed to have been spared publicity. Marissa wondered what the people in St. George were saying. But after a few days, there was nothing else about it. There was more about Christmas, about Christmas concerts, and Christmas books. She was nervous, but when nothing happened, she began to feel the weight of it leave her. The newspaper had made no connections. And the police had been respectfully silent.

Michael and Julie's party on December 23rd was an exciting celebration. It was also the Prophet Joseph Smith's birthday. But two days later, Christmas on the farm was so quiet without Michael or the boys, Marissa took special precautions to get through it. Even Joey had been invited to be with Pam Riddle's family.

Marissa threw up in the morning for the fourth day in a row. She read the Christmas story in the scriptures and nursed her knowledge about the child she was carrying. She tried to lose herself in a Dickens novel, *Little Dorrit,* but couldn't concentrate. She took out the cello and played one of Gounod's elegies. But it made her cry. Finally, she decided to take a walk to the Temple of Sinewava.

Tomorrow, Michael and Julie would drive to Indiana in one of the Robinsons' most reliable automobiles. Michael had already packed and left his valise beside his bassoon at the door. Even his bassoon would be gone. On Marissa's way out, she stopped to glance at it. She had not thought it would affect her to see the instrument lying so inert at the threshold—as though it had once had a life and now sat unmoving, without its spirit. The instrument would never have been alive except in Michael's hands. That was how she felt about herself. She was like an instrument. And without Michael she wondered if she would be as lifeless as the bassoon looked now in the boxy case, coiled in a ruse of outer smiles and goodbyes, but without the one breath that gave it music.

The blue of the sky was the color of Ellen's grandmother's Dresden plate—a milky gauze over the billowing canopy that edged the monoliths surrounding the farm. The air bit Marissa's cheeks when she walked out to the road, and she pulled her scarf up to cover her neck.

"The white throne," she murmured to herself, looking up to it as she stepped across the brown grass. "What did the wolf god, Shinaway, see in it? Isaac Behunin called it the 'Throne of God.' And it looks like some monument carved out of the middle of the earth and raised up to remind us that we are very small."

Indeed, when they were little, she and Michael would put rocks on an ant pile and watch the small creatures scurry about, adjusting to the massive obstacles that blocked the entry to their underground home. Michael lay on his stomach, his chin on his fists. Marissa copied him.

"The workers are going down, making new tunnels," Michael said. "The rocks don't stop them."

"They'll tell the others something's happened to our world," Marissa said. "And they'll all come up and dig around it."

"What if something this big fell on us?" Michael asked.

"We'd just have to work around it."

The road to Sinewava seemed long this Christmas morning, as though she were walking away from the life she knew, and the strings of her heart were holding her back. They were tugging to keep her in the house she knew, with the people she knew, the land she loved. And yet as they pulled, they were pulling it all apart.

Michael was married now. How did he spend his first night? How wonderful would his life be, always in Indiana in the middle of a symphony, in earshot of strains from Schubert and Mendelsohn?

The trees rattled above Marissa on the road, still holding to their dying leaves. Marissa meandered down to the path along the river, shutting her eyes against the needles of light dancing in the water. Looking up, she saw the amazing temple monolith standing alone inside the hollow amphitheater of stones, as though performing some ancient ritual of independence in an arena of red light.

Her uncle Peter had given her mother a cake pan with a hollow cone in the center. Aunt Sophie had said it was to make angel food. Angels could have hollowed out these stones around the temple. If they visited Marissa now in another layer of reality, she honored their presence with her silence.

Glancing off the top of the rock, the light shimmered and sang, seeming to dance with the music of the water. If the flute she and Michael had often heard playing during their duets broke into some amazing arpeggios at this moment, she would not have been surprised.

The angels, the music, the rocks. These stones surrounding her had been here for a long time—and would be here when she and Michael and Julie's grandchildren and great-grandchildren had passed away through layers of air.

"You will stand forever," Marissa murmured. The oblique rays of the winter afternoon carved ridges of shadow on the face of the monument. Dry stalks of sage hung fast to clumps of soil brought by the wind.

"If I could stand alone," Marissa said to herself. "If I were as steady as this rock . . ."

Twenty-three

On Marissa's way back to the house, the wind bit her face. She burrowed into her scarf, but the cold seeped into her sleeves and shoes. She looked at the house. She loved it. Everything about it was connected with wonderful memories of her life.

As she approached the porch, she saw a bright profusion of color sitting by the door. She was surprised to find a basket of fruit in bright yellow tissue paper, sitting on the welcome mat. "Merry Christmas, Marissa, from Bishop and Sister Robinson." She knew it was a gesture of kindness. But she fought the nagging temptation to think that they had taken Michael from her, and all she had left was apples and oranges.

When she opened the door, she saw the boxes and suitcases, including Michael's bassoon, still sitting in the entryway. She wasn't sure if she was relieved or concerned. If he and Julie came back to the house to get the things, would there be another awkward moment with Julie's eyes cast off in the distance, the tendons of her neck tense? But the newlyweds were leaving from the Robinson house in the morning. And Marissa would like to say goodbye—if she could.

She read more of Dickens, this time *A Christmas Carol.* She would let the spirit of Christmas live in her heart all year, learning from the past, the present, and the future. She would never let herself become Scrooge. Or Marley, who had realized after death that mankind was his most important business.

Vowing to love Julie and be a sister to her, Marissa prayed that someday they could be good friends.

When she had almost finished the story—when tears welled up in her eyes because she saw that Scrooge was truly sorry and would change his life—she heard wheels in the driveway. It seemed early. For a young man as smitten as Joey was with Pam Riddle, it was strange he had not wanted to stay a little later with her family.

But it was not Joey. Marissa rose to the window and caught her breath. Michael had come in the Robinsons' car to pick up his belongings.

She leaned against the window frame to steady herself. In the dusky light, she could see he had come alone. She held her breath when the long legs emerged from the driver's side, the lithe body following, and the head of dark hair. When he shut the car door, the sound sent a shudder into her spine. *Michael, Michael, don't you know? There is danger . . .*

Yet she was so glad to see him, she could not quiet the rejoicing of her heart. She flung open the door. "Michael!"

"Marissa!" He was radiant. The enigmatic smile that made a sliver of a moon across his face sent a stab of joy through her body. His eyes flickered with the light she had always seen in them. "Merry Christmas, Marissa!"

She laughed. "It's almost over."

He grinned, looking down from his height at her. "So it is . . . Did you get . . . ?" Once inside the house, he glanced around and found the fruit the Robinsons had brought. "Oh, good, you got it! The bishop wanted to invite you to dinner, but . . ."

"I understand." Marissa smiled.

"Joey went to the Riddles'."

"Yes."

"He is quite taken with Pam. It's good for him."

"I'm happy," Marissa said.

"Well, I will take all of this off your hands." Michael stood over the bassoon, the boxes, and the case.

"I'll help," she said.

"Oh, they're too heavy. I should be able to get them in a couple of trips."

"No. I can carry the little boxes. I can even carry the bassoon."

She picked up a small box and held it while he jimmied the largest case into his arms.

In a few minutes everything was packed into the trunk and the back seat, and all that was left was the bassoon. They stood over it in the entryway.

"I didn't want to leave you alone, Marissa," Michael said. "Joey told me everything. I want you to know that . . . but I don't know . . . something in Julie. She doesn't want . . . She's just happier if I don't talk about you or if she pretends you are no longer in my life."

Marissa stood frozen by the hall mirror. Her heart beat hard, and she feared she might cry.

"She senses how I feel about you," he said.

"And to her I am an intruder. I understand."

Michael paused and looked down. The bassoon still lay on the floor. "I'm not sure I understand, Marissa. You— you have no idea how much I . . ."

The air was becoming thick with the dusk flowing around them. Marissa said nothing.

"You know that true love . . . well, we're taught . . . that true love—" Michael was stammering. "True love is the love we share with everyone."

Marissa did not speak.

"Well, even the love between a man and a woman. You can love more than one person . . ."

Marissa knew what he was saying. And it was true. She stayed so silent, the darkness seemed to ring in the distant hills.

"We were careful," Michael said, then stopped. "I'm not saying this very well."

Marissa's heart leaped. "Michael, I love you. I will always love you. This feeling that I have for you now, this love, it is so beautiful to me that if I never feel it again in this life for anyone else . . ." For a moment there was silence. "I believe it was you I loved when I reached out in the impossible situation and pretended it was the real thing." She tossed her head back and laughed a little. "I didn't like marriage. It was just painful. All I really wanted all my life was to feel what I feel for you—even if only for a short time, Michael." *Michael, Michael, Michael.*

His eyes clouded over. "If I . . . if I tell you something, Marissa . . . I cried out your name in my sleep." The quiet was louder than she could ever remember. "She heard it."

No wonder Julie wanted nothing to do with her.

For that moment beside the open door that would close over him in a few moments, there was a wave of music that seemed to come out of the hills. It was cold, but it had never been so cold in Zion that the warmth of the colors didn't echo for joy.

"If I don't write much, it will be because I am trying to make the life I have committed to live the best it can possibly be." His eyes began to glisten. It was obvious he was struggling.

Marissa raised her hand. With the back of it, she brushed his cheek.

A sob rose in Michael's throat, and he reached out and drew her into his arms. She responded—oh, how she responded. Her heart hammered in her breast. The atmosphere burst with so much fire. "I don't know why things work out the way they do," he whispered in her hair. "All we can do is honor our commitments, and trust . . ."

She began to sob. The tears rolled down her cheeks. She gasped to hold them back. For a moment every sound that had ever echoed in the canyon seemed to rise into an unparalleled symphony that can be understood only by those who have found love—even if only for a moment. Marissa believed she would never feel this way again. And if that were true, this instant was enough to refer to for the rest of her life.

"I love you, Michael. Never forget it."

He was sobbing unashamedly. He held her so close she could feel his body trembling. She did not know how long they stood there, feeding each other so much joy.

She drew back and put the palm of her hand against his cheek. "This is what love is," she whispered, "wanting the best for everyone."

But she would never deny that she wanted him. She wanted him with every beat of her heart. She heard that music in her veins, the cry that separation from the only one she had ever loved would tear her in two.

"Just remember," she whispered. "We have had something very few in this world have ever had. A love that is so sure and so real that it will never die."

She pulled away from the fire that loomed close in their embrace.

"Don't they say"—Marissa gave a little laugh— "it is better to have loved and lost than never to have loved at all?"

Michael's eyes were filled with tears. "I'd better go now," he whispered. "All . . . all I really wanted to do was . . . say goodbye."

She smiled. "We can't say goodbye. We are alive in the breath of each others' spirits." She pulled away to see him clearly. “We are so much a part of each other. Don’t you believe we will live together forever, even apart?”

“Marissa,” he said, looking away from her. “Oh, Marissa. I— I don’t know what—”

“You love Julie. Make her happy.”

“Yes,” he said. He took Marissa’s hands in both of his and kissed them. “Marissa, you are amazing. Be happy too.”

The sound of the Robinsons’ Buick echoed against the Watchman. She could hear it long after it left the curve of the road at the Steamboat Rock. She heard its swift exit from Zion. And she shut the door.

My mother, Marissa, never held back any information from me about who my father was, or what happened to cause her to lose track of him so completely. Even when she married John Cohen, the father I came to love so much before he died, I believed I knew all that transpired in her life.

I was born in Salt Lake City while she was getting her master’s degree at the University of Utah. My earliest memories were of Aunt Sophie and Uncle Peter walking around the block with me in the president streets, saying hello to the neighbors and bringing bits of old breakfast sausage to Mr. Parsifal’s dog, Trap. He was a big German shepherd with a wet nose. Once or twice, if I felt very brave, I reached out and touched that nose, then pulled back and shook my hands.

When I married Steve, we moved to Massachusetts and didn’t keep up with the things that took place in Utah. I talked with my mother on the telephone. She made some visits, and my family visited when we could. I thought I knew most of what she was doing while she was teaching at the university, and while

John was ill. We came back to Utah for his funeral, and visited with his family and Joey's family at the park.

When my mother retired, she sold the real-estate holdings John and the children from his first marriage left her, returned to St. George, and built a beautiful home near Joey, who had married Pam and had a houseful of children. In 1931 he had relinquished the farm to the government and purchased a successful furniture store in nearby Washington City. With the money from the real estate, and what was left of the sale of the farm, my mother spent a long time creating a beautiful house on the brow of a hill looking east over the blue and gold desert landscape into the barely visible Zion that she loved. She took painting classes and danced with the senior citizens.

She told me a little about Michael Rosefield. She said she had always yearned to establish more contact with him and his family. Though both of them were married, she believed it would be all right to try to find him after all this time. She heard from him then, once or twice. But always just postcards, and no return address. Joey told her the family lived in California, where Michael taught music at a prominent university. He and Julie had three beautiful daughters.

When I was helping my mother move to St. George, I couldn't help looking at some of her letters. I saw the postcards from Michael, one of a Swiss village describing a trip he and Julie took to Switzerland. Another time, he sent a photograph of himself with all of the wind instruments he had learned to play. It was not until years later that I learned how hard my mother had tried to renew her contact with one of the people of her life who had definitely been a favorite friend.

Twenty-four

While Marissa was busy with her husband John and his children and grandchildren, as well as her daughter Sunny's family, she heard from Joey that he had finally found Michael's address. Excited, Marissa told John that at last she had found how to contact her brother Michael. She wanted to see if they could get together. Patient and understanding, John was amenable to the suggestion, but when she wrote to Michael, she was surprised how they began to open up to each other. She found herself saying how she truly felt about things—as though she had kept it bottled up in her heart all these years. She was also thrilled to receive letters from him that expressed warmth and yearning. She wrote:

> *Remember Zion, Michael? It was so beautiful it has left a signature on my heart that has marked all the years of my life. Returning to it reminds me of you. I long to see you and your family.*

He wrote back:

> *I can't believe it, Marissa. Amazing! You are still alive! When I got your letter in the mail I was taken back. I have thought of you so many times and wondered what you were doing, and how you were. I still can't believe we are in touch again.*

Marissa wrote:

On a recent trip to Zion, all I could hear was our music in the river and in the stones. I could not play or listen to music for seven years after I lost you. But I married a nice widower. I helped raise his family, along with my wonderful daughter, Sunny, who blessed my life.

I have never forgotten you. I have always prayed in my heart that you found happiness in your life.

Michael responded.

Dear Marissa,

We are doing well. We have three daughters and seven grandchildren. I've retired. Julie is the president of our homeowners' association's garden club. We're both healthy, playing tennis and going to football games.

For a time, the old siblings recalled their years together and enjoyed catching up on their activities. But soon the letters began to take on an unusual heat. Marissa was surprised at how strong the feelings resonated in her heart.

We missed out on a good friendship all of these years—on sharing our families, on sharing our past, our love for one another, and the poignant experiences of our past. I still love you so much, Michael.

As the letters progressed, Marissa begged him to bring his family to Utah. Her hope intensified. And the fact that he responded to her brought her so much joy. But Michael was very much aware of how circumspect both of them must be.

And then one day, a letter Marissa had sent to him came back unopened. Sprawled across the top of it, in Julie's beautiful but emphatic penmanship, was the message RETURN TO SENDER. Following this missive came a formidable special-delivery package, marked clearly that it was from both Michael and Julie. Each of them had written to her. Marissa read Michael's letter first. And when she did, she knew she would never read what Julie had to say.

I kept your letters, and Julie found them and read them all. She was terribly upset. I am in danger of losing my family. What you and I are sharing now is wrong. This has been a very difficult time. You and I both have good lives. We must forget one another and move forward. Everything you send to me will be returned without being opened. Please do not communicate with me again in any way, shape, or form.

Marissa put both of the letters away, not even glancing at Julie's. Sobbing, holding Michael's letter away from her so she would not read all of it, so that the terrible words would not carve themselves indelibly into her memory, she wrote in her journal:

Michael. All my life I searched for something I felt was missing. It was you. I know this, because in talking to you in these few letters we have shared, I have felt more love than I have ever felt in my life. It is fire, it is grace, it is life itself. And now that I have found it once again and have captured it in my heart, I can truly say, "It is better to have loved and lost than never to have loved at all."

I love you, Michael. It is real, it is lasting, it is eternal. And if the heavens are just, I will see you at the seat of God.

Epilogue

When Marissa lost Michael, she lost music. She sold her cello and never played it again. But when John died and she moved to her lovely home in St. George, she took up her drawing and painting with enthusiasm, mostly creating pictures of the park. Finally, she began to sell little drawings and watercolor sketches of Zion in the shops of Springdale and Hurricane. She often took her sketch pad with her up the trails to Weeping Rock or the Narrows. She would unpack her paint box, sit on her little camp stool, get out her paints, and make the canyon come alive on paper or canvas. After she learned to paint portraits, she began doing commissioned work for wealthy families. Art galleries gave her space to show her paintings, and soon she was garnering awards.

Once she finished discharging her responsibilities toward Joey's family or her Church callings, Marissa often drove to the park and hiked the trails with her paint box and easel to capture the light in the early morning and late afternoon. As the sun settled over the Patriarchs, she would sit at the new visitors' center and paint the sky and the monoliths she loved.

One of her favorite trails was to Emerald Pools. On a warm Saturday one September, she carried her paint box and easel and walked up through the winding rocks that flanked the small pathway through the amazing colors of the moss, the red and gold autumn leaves.

Ahead of her on this day, she saw an older, white-haired gentleman walking alone. The tilt of his head forward, his shoulders, the long legs—all seemed familiar to her. When he turned slightly to round the bend, she saw his face. It was Michael! She knew it was. Her heart stopped for a moment. She felt weak. *Michael.* It had been a lifetime.

For a few seconds she could not breathe. But she gulped and continued walking, watching to make sure. As she came around the bend, she saw ahead of him a family, with two small boys and a little girl running up one side of the trail, clapping, skipping, and shouting. The girl suddenly ran back to the tall, elderly gentleman and grabbed his hand. "Grandpa, hurry! You can see the big fountain."

The mother and father were walking ahead, holding hands.

One of the boys raced back to hurry his sister, then said, "Grandpa! Go faster! You're as slow as Grandma used to be when she was alive!"

The third and smallest of the children ran ahead to his parents.

Marissa's heart lurched against her ribs. She slowed her step, observing until the magnificent weeping falls suddenly loomed over them. She held her paint box closely against her chest, feeling how solid it was, because she would need something to hang onto.

She tried to catch her breath. To her right, below the trail, was the spot where Bird's old cabin had once been. The government had razed it many years ago when they built the huge visitors' center, complete with museum, shop, and lecture rooms where park rangers helped the public understand how these magnificent monoliths came to be, and why everyone in the world wanted to see them. The memories washed over Marissa.

The trail was so narrow that unless she turned around now and hurried in the opposite direction, she would meet the family face to face on their way back down.

She filled her lungs with air. The sun was playing in the mist that rose from the pools. She walked forward.

About the Author

Marilyn McMeen Brown hopes to illuminate Mormon culture for outsiders, whose perception of that faith is so often in error. Zion National Park's spectacular beauty can only be matched by the strength of character in its historic Christian residents. It is these people and their honorable lives this novel explores.

Marilyn has written more than a dozen novels, as well as five histories, two stage musicals, and five books of poetry. She has won state and local writing awards for her fiction. She eulogizes her background not only in her writing, but in her commitment to her beliefs, her culture, and her family life with husband Bill and their six children, eighteen grandchildren, and four great-grandchildren.

For more information about Marilyn and her books, please visit www.marilynbrownauthor.com.